Christmas at Whispering Creek

Barbara M. Britton

Cover Art by *Nicola Martinez*
White Rose Publishing, a division of Pelican Ventures, LLC
www.pelicanbookgroup.com PO Box 1738 *Aztec, NM * 87410
White Rose Publishing Circle and Rosebud logo is a trademark of Pelican Ventures, LLC

Publishing History
First White Rose Edition, 2022
Paperback Edition ISBN 978-1-5223-0395-4
Electronic Edition ISBN 978-1-5223-0394-7
Published in the United States of America

What People are Saying

Fans of Christian romance will laugh and cry while reading this heartfelt Christmas story gracefully written by the talented Barbara Britton!

~ Laura Scott, USA Today Bestselling Author

Barbara Britton is a master at writing Christian fiction. In *Christmas at Whispering Creek*, she has written a powerful story of overcoming loss, both physical and emotional. Of forgiveness and second chances. Of running toward God, rather than running away— especially in the hard times. *Christmas at Whispering Creek* is a compelling story of finding wholeness through brokenness.

~Carol James, best-selling author

Christmas at Whispering Creek is a departure from Barbara Britton's usual Biblical fiction genre, but she nails it with this moving story of depending on God through trials, making life a little brighter for others, and finding a happily ever after.

~Karen Malley, author of the Pine Springs Series

1

Samantha Williams parked her mid-size SUV and hopped out into a forty-six-degree December day. The length of her lunch break at the florist shop, and the proximity of her boyfriend's apartment, made walking his obstinate beagle a breeze. She grabbed Buddy's well-chewed leash and jogged across the courtyard in her puffy coat and comfortable boots.

After unlocking the apartment door, she dipped down to stop the routine jailbreak of her walking partner. Why hadn't she heard the scratch of his paws? Had Buddy shut himself in the bathroom again? No clammy nose or rough tongue greeted her palm. She glanced around the living room.

Movement by the bedroom door caught her eye. Heat shot through her veins. Someone was in the apartment. She gripped the leash in case she'd need to use it as a whip. What was she thinking? *Run.*

"Sam," a familiar voice rumbled.

Her heart almost imploded as her boyfriend strode from his bedroom, walking between the leather sofa and special-order coffee table. She blew out a gust of relief. "Karlton. What are you doing here?" She placed a hand over her chest and tried to calm her booming heart. "I didn't expect you until tomorrow. You almost had the clip of Buddy's leash embedded in your forehead." She rushed forward to give him a hug. Maybe he wanted to surprise her? The law firm interview in Chicago must have gone well for him to be home a day early.

She wrapped her arms around Karlton's light blue oxford shirt and breathed in his understated musk cologne. His body stiffened. He patted her shoulder as if she were Buddy bothering him during a study binge. Was he afraid of hurting her? Or crushing her prosthetic breast?

Pulling away, she smiled as bright as the Wisconsin winter sun. Perhaps, his interview was a bust. Karlton had his heart set on that firm. She knew the feeling of being underemployed.

"I'm glad you're here." Karlton scrubbed a hand over his jaw, but his lips did not curve into a happy-to-see-you smile.

His flatline exuberance was underwhelming. She gripped the dog leash and glanced around for her four-legged charge. Moving boxes were stacked in the corner of the kitchenette. Boxes she would have noticed yesterday when she played with Buddy. A high-pitched hum like a guitar solo from a metal band lodged in her ears.

"You're moving?" She stumbled backward. How long had he been making plans to leave? "You must have gotten a job offer?"

"I did." The joyous news didn't dimple his cheeks. "I'll be swapping Milwaukee for the Chicago law scene. I can start at Pearce, Sutton while I finish my last class online. They'll even mentor me for the bar exam."

She should have listened to her inner voice earlier and ran. Now, she was stuck staring at her soulmate and his soul seemed distracted with everything but her. What was he really doing during the time he spent preparing for interviews?

Karlton stared at the wall.

Samantha turned to see what held his attention.

His gaze was focused on a spider's web dangling from the ceiling. "I start in two weeks. And I found a condo near the office."

She swallowed, her throat constricting on her pride. No invitation to join him burst forth. "That's wonderful." Wonderfully convenient.

His mouth gaped as if he were formulating an argument.

"When were you going to tell me?" Pressure throbbed behind her eyes. "As you were filling out change of address cards?" Her voice squeaked with a pathetic whine.

"I could have texted." Karlton grinned halfheartedly and shoved his hands in his couture slacks.

"A text?" Hysteria bubbled beneath her words. "Written like one of your lawyer's briefs? I took tomorrow off so we could have a long weekend together." She and Karlton used to go on long walks by the lake before medical procedures got in the way. Those lazy days seemed like a decade ago.

"Samantha." He rocked forward, his gaze darting to the leash in her hand. "You knew I might be leaving.

This is my future."

Muted barking began from the apartment next door. She knew that chastising bark. Her eyes grew wide at the realization of who was watching Buddy.

"Buddy's at your neighbor's? With the chatty barista?" She dropped the leash onto his wooden floor. The metal clasp clacked on the polished plank. Rubbing her forehead, she willed herself not to break down. Deep in her heart she knew he had been growing distant. The studying. Exam prep. Graduation in the spring. Lining up interviews. Or. Oh, no, not that. Her diagnosis had a long tail. "It's the cancer, isn't it? You want someone whole." Darn if a tear didn't escape her lashes and slide down her cheek.

"Of course not. It's just—" He shuffled toward her, lifeless. His affections were already residing with the pretty woman who wore stilettos, dyed her hair blonde, and lived a wall away. "I'm sorry, Sam. But we're in different places right now. I have to do what's best for me."

No, don't be nice. Her lone tear had invited friends to a dance party all over her face.

"I understand." She bobbed her head. What man wanted a scarred girlfriend? "We haven't seen each other much. It's just…I thought I'd have some warning. You know. Realize the end was coming." She'd made excuses for his absences. In a deep recess of her heart, she admitted he had been trying to break free ever since breast cancer left its ugly mark.

Karlton opened his arms.

What did he think? Another pathetic hug would

help? She raced for the door to escape and prayed she caught the knob through the wavy ocean of her vision.

"Bye, Buddy," she said as she raced past the peep hole of blondie's place.

"I did love you, Samantha," Karlton called from the doorway, his confession lingering in the crisp air.

When? Before my breast cancer? When I was whole? She couldn't answer. Not when her lips were trembling, and her nose was dripping onto her zipped-up coat. *Why, Lord? Why are you taking everything from me?*

She fumbled the keys in her pocket and opened the door to her car with one press of the fob.

Pull it together, Sam. She laughed. How would she hide her mottled complexion from her boss? Hide her face behind a hydrangea? A throb of embarrassment seasoned with anger threatened to overtake her. In the midst of her own surgeries and radiation, she had been a source of encouragement to Karlton during his classes and interviews. What a waste of energy. She swiped at her runny nose and closed the car door.

Her cell phone buzzed in its holder. Surely, it wasn't Karlton. "He'd text," she mocked. Squinting at the caller display, she read Lynch, Siebold, and Lee. Was that a law firm on Karlton's list? One of his top contenders? Did they want a reference? Oh, she would give them a reference. Sniffing as if to dry the ocean, she blew out a breath and answered.

"Hello." Her greeting sounded semi-steady even if she was the sole judge.

"Is this Samantha Williams?" a baritone voice

asked.

This guy sounded older, like a senior partner. "Yes, this is Samantha. May I ask who's calling?" Her mom would be pleased with her professionalism.

"Chester Siebold. I'm an attorney calling about…"

Karlton Two-timer.

"Theodore Beckman."

She sat straighter and swept her hair away from her ear and the phone. "Wait. You're calling about Mr. Ted?"

"Yes. I represent his estate."

"His estate? You mean, Mr. Ted is…" Could the lump in her throat get any bigger? "Has died…?"

"I'm so sorry, Miss Williams." The gentleman had more compassion in his condolences than her boyfriend had in his ditch of their relationship. Correction. Former boyfriend. "He passed away three weeks ago of a heart attack. I thought you had heard by now." The attorney coughed. "You aren't driving, are you?"

"No, no I'm not." Little did he know this was her second blow of the day, and she hadn't eaten lunch. Her mom always said that things came in threes. What was next? Another spot on her mammogram? She refused to go there. "Mr. Ted, um, Theodore was my next-door neighbor when I was growing up." No wonder she hadn't heard anything from Ted recently. She swallowed the taste of rotten egg that had settled in her mouth.

"I was wondering if you could come to Whispering Creek. Mr. Beckman named you in his estate. There's a fairly large bequest, and I have paperwork to go over with you."

If Mr. Ted left her enough money, maybe she could pay off her medical bills and student loans. Ted had been kind to her all of her life. His wife, too. A sob wracked her chest. She chastised herself for letting her mind think of money over people.

"How…how far away is that?" Her words stuck as she stopped a sob. Ted had moved to Tennessee, but she had never calculated the distance. She cleared her throat and asked again. "How far is the drive to Whispering Creek from Milwaukee?"

As the attorney answered, Samantha glimpsed Karlton and the barista strolling in the distance. Their hands were clasped, and Buddy pulled on his leash haphazardly sniffing the boxwood bushes. Karlton's interview prep must have gone well with a late-night cappuccino or latte. At the moment, Tennessee wasn't far enough away for this Wisconsin cheese head.

~*~

"Mom, I'll be OK." Samantha folded a pair of jeans and laid it in the suitcase opened on her bed. Her mother leaned against the doorframe. Moving back home after the reconstruction surgery failed seemed like a prudent idea at the time. Free rent. Few expenses. Nurse on call. Except her mom never went off duty even when she wasn't working at the hospital. "I have directions from the attorney, a GPS, and a cell phone. It's only a day's drive. I'll be fine."

Her mom pulled at the neck of her sweater. "Did you talk to your father?"

"Yes, and he asked if I had a full tank of gas, bottled water, and a jug of salt for icy conditions." Sam wedged a small round box into the corner of the suitcase. The container was a comfy home for her prosthetic breast. After underwear and socks were added to her wardrobe, she strolled to the doorway of her bedroom and hugged her mom.

"Are you sure you don't want Dad and I to go?" Her mom's words tickled Sam's chest. "I only want to help."

Sam smiled to calm her mother's fears. "I know, Mom. I promise if I need any help, I'll call. Mr. Siebold assured me we'll connect with you and Dad if I have any questions or need advice. I'm able to sign documents on my own at twenty-three."

"But I worry." Her mom sniffled. "Especially since Karlton—"

"Somehow, I suspected the end was coming. I'll be fine," Sam assured her mother. Darn if her fake breast didn't feel as if it had gained ten pounds. "The drive will do me good. I'll have time to process all of that." She eased out of her mother's embrace and grinned as if a table of presents waited to be opened. "Think of it as my early Christmas break. Besides, it's almost sixty degrees down south. A heat wave with no snowstorms or iced pavement."

"Can I put you on the prayer chain?" Her mom headed into the hallway and halted. "Many at church remember Mr. Ted. They know we were close. They'll want to lift you up in prayer. Especially for travel mercies."

"Sure, you can add me." Sam zipped her suitcase and hefted it onto the floor. "If you don't think they're tired of praying for my issues." Two surgeries. Radiation. Infection. Her health problems had family friends on their knees for weeks. No, months. They should be called the knee pad brigade.

Her mom headed down the hall. The squeak from the catch-all drawer in the kitchen broke the silence. When her mom returned, she held out several twenty-dollar bills. "Take this hundred in case of an emergency."

Shaking her head, Sam took the money. Anything to calm her mother's fears, which had been plenty of late. Sam wasn't worried about driving to Tennessee and meeting an attorney. Mr. Ted's remembrance of the little girl who grew up playing in his yard and attending his Sunday school class was a blessing. A blessing she needed right now more than ever. She didn't expect another life emergency to occur in Whispering Creek.

2

Cole Donoven lounged in a chair on a sunny beach with a cool glass bottle in his hand. An annoying gull squawked nearby and stamped a pattern into the sand with its webbed feet. Faint buzzing caught his attention and the seabird's. Bothered by the reverberating hum, the noisy gull darted away.

Opening his eyes, Cole realized he'd been dreaming. What he wouldn't give to have his toes submerged in warm sand again. Light glowed beneath the white sheet on the other side of the bed. Who would be calling this early? Or was it early? He rolled over and glanced at the clock on the nightstand. His mother insisted the day and time display would be helpful. She was right. He knew it was Saturday, ten minutes after seven, and the third of December. His phone stopped bothering him. Good. He couldn't think of anyone he wanted to talk to anyway, not with his temples throbbing and demanding a large cup of caffeine.

Kicking the comforter away from his feet, he sat on the edge of the bed and pulled on some boxer briefs. His phone came alive again. He slid the phone from under the sheet and saw Stephen Slater's number scrolling across the screen. Of course, his manager was calling. The guy was good at picking scabs and blowing up phones. Cole answered and prepared for his headache to become a migraine.

"Hey, Donoven." His music manager's words were as smooth as coffee creamer. "You haven't been takin' my calls."

Cole shuffled to the kitchen. The wood floor chilled his bare feet. "Been busy." At absolutely nothing.

"Writing another song?" Slater's tone was the usual bubble-wrapped razor blade.

"Why don't you ask Jillie Lynn about that." Cole grabbed a mug from the sink and poured yesterday's coffee into it. "She got me into this."

Slater's sigh rivaled the microwave's motor. "I can't get a hold of JL."

"What? They don't have 5G in Ireland?" Cole removed the lukewarm mug and sipped his stale coffee, hoping it would calm the ache in his head. "Can't her famous squeeze afford an international plan?"

"Hey, man. I'm sorry about the way that went down." His manager did sound sympathetic. "I had no idea they were a thing until she left with him on the tour. I have enough to keep track of without delving into people's personal lives."

Cole swallowed a mouthful of brown mud and pondered a response. Slater wasn't the one who'd stomped on his heart with rhinestone cowgirl boots. Cole kicked himself for not realizing Jillie Lynn's flirty, sweet talk landed on whoever was within reach.

Collaborating on songs had been her idea, not his.

"It's only one more song." Slater's groveling began. "Complete the contract, and I'll owe you big. I have faith in you."

Did he even want to keep composing honky-tonk heartbreak choruses? Or wronged girlfriend vengeance anthems? Could he even complete a song without JL? A cramp clenched low in his gut. He had worried about Jillie Lynn the first time he saw her lugging her guitar case late at night in a questionable part of Nashville. He should have worried more about his heart and sanity. "When do you need it by, considering my muse is traveling the world?"

"Find another muse. I need it by Christmas." An annoying pencil drumming filtered through the phone. "What about that retreat place you and JL went last summer?"

"It was someone's log house." Cole stuck his mouth under the faucet and washed the grit from yesterday's coffee out of his mouth. "And there are memories there." An image of a sunset and a simmering stolen kiss flashed through his mind. He almost choked as he swallowed the last gulp of water.

"Make new memories. I've never missed a deadline, and I don't want to start now. My reputation means something in this industry." Here came the sharp blade. "Your reputation should mean something to you, too. Or at least, I thought it did."

Slater sounded too much like Cole's dad. Well, he wasn't.

"Do you hear me?" His manager was like a pit bull

tugging on a week-old sock.

"Loud and clear." Cole bent down to get a frying pan out of the cupboard. "I'll think of something soon and send it your way. Catch you later." He ended the call before Slater made any more demands. Slater's understanding and compassion evaporated as soon as it left his lips.

Cole heated the frying pan and cracked three eggs onto the non-stick surface. Could he write a song without Jillie Lynn? She was the real artist. Is that why she left? He hadn't pulled his weight? Didn't play guitar like a pro? Couldn't finish a lyric? Wasn't good enough for her gold record elites? *Don't go down her avenue of insults.*

Flipping his eggs, he added a bit of salt, pepper, and sriracha and scooped his breakfast onto a plate. Slouching at the kitchenette table, he licked egg from the tines of his fork, and let the burn of the hot sauce fill his mouth. A daily devotional rested next to his silverware. His mom sent the booklets every month. Mostly, they made it into the recycling bin without being read. Philippians 4:13 was written on the cover in his mom's loopy handwriting. *I can do everything through Christ who gives me strength.*

Right now, he needed all the strength he could get. Life had done a fast turn on bald tires, and he didn't have any tread left to grip the road. Would Ted have spare rooms he could use again to hang out and write? He flung his fork onto the table. He only needed one room this time, but he would compose something for himself and something good enough for Slater.

An hour later, when he had showered and shaved, he threw a duffle bag into his truck. After wedging his guitar case behind the driver's seat, he drove west. Away from Nashville. Away from interruptions. And away from the memory of a woman who had discarded him like a gooey gum wrapper.

He prayed Whispering Creek still knew how to whisper a song.

3

After a warm, yet professional greeting from Chester Siebold, Samantha perched on the edge of an overstuffed leather chair, facing an impressively large wooden desk and a wall of bookcases. Perfectly aligned legal volumes made a nice backdrop. Clutching a disposable cup, she sipped the caffeinated coffee, willing her eyes to stay open. Nine o'clock was too early to decipher estate terminology after driving most of yesterday and crashing last night in a nearby motel.

Thank heavens, Ted's lawyer agreed to meet her on a Saturday. She tugged on her sweater dress to cover more of her black leggings. Hopefully, the meeting would go smoothly, and she could be back on her way to Wisconsin. Life had been too unpredictable of late with breakups, cancelled teacher contracts, and oncology follow ups. She hoped for a pre-cancer normal to return soon.

The attorney, who had asked her to call him Chester, squinted over his reading glasses at a document. He cleared his throat and quivered his double chin. "Ted Beckman has left you a substantial gift. You have inherited his property which has a log home on it. The lot designation is explained in this paragraph." He turned the trust paperwork her direction and noted the writing with a gold-tipped pen. "The plat survey will show the area and boundary lines."

A surge of adrenaline cleared the morning fog from her brain. Property? "Mr. Ted left me his house?" How would she take care of property in another state? Would she have to pay taxes? Or was money included? Karlton could have helped her with the legal questions if he hadn't dumped her before he jetted off to work for big law in Chicago. No, she wouldn't think about that two-timer. Unlike her former boyfriend, Mr. Ted had always been there for her. He'd called and given her advice when she'd set up her first classroom, e-mailed her old lesson plans, and shared how to best use the resource room. Ted treated her like the child he never had, but this generosity was more than all his birthday presents and graduation gifts combined.

She wiped a tear from her eye and set her coffee cup on the side table. "Wow. I'm in shock. I mean...I never expected Ted to leave me his house." She needed money to pay medical bills, not property requiring upkeep. Although knowing Ted, his house would be pristine. His late wife, Nan, always kept a tidy home. "I'm not ungrateful." *I sure sound like it.* "It's, um, I don't have a lot of income right now. I work part-time in a floral shop." Instead of teaching a classroom of second graders. *Thank you, cancer.* She laced her fingers and tried to keep the shaking to a minimum. Would this inheritance add to her debt?

Chester held up a well-manicured hand and

grinned. "I imagine the last thing you expected was to be a homeowner in Tennessee."

The idea wasn't even on her one-in-a-million-chance list.

"Let me assure you, Miss. Williams, there are funds designated to pay the taxes and a small gift as well. You could use those funds for moving expenses or for remodeling the property."

She nodded, but finding an apartment, moving out of her parent's house, discovering career opportunities, having a possible reconstruction surgery, those were on her to-do list, not relocating to the South. Did they even have a hospital and top-in-their-field oncologists in Whispering Creek? "Could I sell it?" Her chest ached as she voiced the idea. Would Ted be disappointed in her?

"You could. Once we get the title transferred." Chester steepled his fingertips and relaxed in his seat. The leather squeaked under the shift in his weight. "Once you visit the home, you may decide otherwise." His voice held a renewed energy as though he was leading a jury. "Let me show you the aerial photos. They're on my secretary's desk." He rose and exited his office.

Maybe she should have allowed one of her parents to come to the meeting for support. They had settled her great aunt's estate. This inheriting business was all new. Her phone vibrated in her purse. She removed it and glanced at the display. Emma, her bestie, was calling. Emma would speak some wisdom to the situation. "Hey," Sam whispered. "I'm in the attorney's office. He stepped out to get some papers."

"Well, I'm glad you made it there safely. You were a zombie on the phone last night."

"Ten hours of highway driving will do that. But guess what?"

"What?"

"You won't believe this. Mr. Ted left me his house."

"Whoa. Spring break at your place." Emma's exuberant laughter reverberated in Sam's ear.

"Funny, Em, but I don't know if I'm going to keep it." Her support system lived and breathed in Wisconsin.

"Why not? It's not like you have a house of your own." Emma spoke in her investment strategist voice. "You were just talking about moving out from your parent's place."

"Yeah, but I wanted to stay in the same zip code."

"Hey, we've been praying for God to give you direction. Don't shut down this opportunity too fast. Just sayin'."

The office door swung open.

Sam bent to put the phone away. "I've got to go. Everything's surreal."

"Call me later. And send pictures. Keep an open mind. OK?"

"I will. For you." Sam ended the call. She'd take lots of pictures for Emma and for Mom and Dad, too. They'd be curious about the inheritance. She slipped her phone back in her purse and contemplated owning a home outright at twenty-three.

Chester unfurled what looked like a large map onto his desk. The opening of the paper sounded like a soft rumble of thunder.

She stood to get a better look at the landscape. Brushing her hair behind her ear, she willed herself not to cry and drip on the images. Mr. Ted wasn't around anymore to give her his wise counsel and a huge bear hug.

"This is a survey of the area. Here's the road and the creek." The attorney swept his finger along the pictures. "There's a shared access road onto the property. Mr. Beckman's brother owns this acreage. You own the acreage on the other side of the common road." Chester circled the picture of Ted's house with his index finger.

Whoa. She blinked as she scanned the property. Her inheritance wasn't a square home on a city block with a patch of grass and neighbors next door. Before her was the most extravagant gift anyone had ever given her. Her throat grew tight. She would trade the log house and land for one more dinner of grilled brats and sauerkraut with Ted and Nan. "That's…"

"A nice piece of property." Chester sounded as though he was making a declaration in court. He assessed her over the top of his readers and quirked a bushy eyebrow.

She pointed at groves of pine trees near the log house. "I didn't realize there'd be so many trees." At least she didn't have to worry about mowing grass if she stayed.

"I think decades ago, someone had their sights on

this being a tree farm, including Christmas trees." Chester smoothed the gray hair at his temples. "Nobody built a house on the property until Ted bought it."

"So, this was going to be a Christmas tree farm?" Emma would love it. Her friend would want to decorate every pine.

"At one time. Now I think Ted's brother has some ATV trails that the locals use." Her attorney pointed to an area on the other side of the lane. "The trails start closer to Ernie's residence."

Great. A reason why Ernie should have inherited this land. "Well, I never saw Ted on an ATV."

Chester laughed. "Me, neither. You can't chance a rollover at eighty-four."

Sam licked her lips. "Why didn't Ted leave the land to his brother?" Ted had always treated her as if she was his own daughter. Perhaps he was still trying to take care of her. *God, I don't know what to do.* The last thing she needed was a family dispute. "I don't suppose you could tell me if Ted's brother inherited something?" If she ever needed a lawyer, she would call Chester because his face didn't twitch, pull, or grin.

"Earnest Beckman was taken care of nicely."

Savings? Life insurance? Teacher pension? IRAs? She would have preferred to receive money to pay off her medical bills and start fresh in a new apartment. Why did Ted think leaving her land next to his brother was a good idea? She barely knew Ted's brother. Her oncologist wanted her to limit the stress in her life. Now, her mind was filled with questions. Would she have to clean out the property? Or the house? What about Ted's effects? She rubbed her temple as pain shot across her forehead. She should have eaten more for breakfast than the motel's free toaster pastry and pink kiddie yogurt. She forced a grateful smile. "I'm glad Ted remembered his brother. Though, wouldn't Earnest have been able to take care of the house? Rent it out and keep an eye on it?"

Chester dipped his double chin and gave her a stare that would have innocent people confessing to a crime. "Have you met Ted's brother?"

"Once or twice. When I was in grade school. He and his wife came to Milwaukee for a vacation." She didn't remember any recent visits before Ted relocated. After Nan died, Ted decided to move closer to his brother. Ted had bought the house two years prior. "Ted came here to be near family, I think." Was that a lie? She rubbed her palms on her leggings. "Ted and Nan didn't take many trips during the school year. They were both teachers. I was too busy with friends in the summer to track their travels." Her parents could have added more details if they had come along. "Um, does Earnest know about me inheriting the land and house?"

Chester nodded. "I hope by now Ernie's digested the information."

Her stomach could use an antacid coating at the moment.

Indicating for her to sit down, Chester grabbed a file folder. "I have a few papers to go over with you, and then I'll take you out to the house. I would have contacted you sooner, but I was out of town when Ted passed. Dealing with Ernie, well..." He gave her a grandfatherly smile. "I'm very sorry for your loss, but perhaps this nice Christmas gift will ease some of your grief."

He wasn't kidding. Ted had given her an unexpected and lavish Christmas present, but it was hundreds of miles away from her home. If she sold the property, would she betray Ted's last wishes? The selling price would launch her nicely in Milwaukee, but would she be plagued by guilt? *Lord, what path have You set me on?*

A little later, Sam followed Chester's car with the license plate CRT DOC out of Whispering Creek proper and into the less populated countryside. Groves of pine trees separated clear cut fields. A few raindrops fell from the light gray sky, enough to streak her dusty windshield. Her phone rang in its cupholder. Her mom was calling. Sam had no doubt both of her parents were waiting for her to answer. Mom didn't work at the hospital on weekends, and Dad was free on Saturdays unless a computer system crashed. She pressed the answer button.

"Hey, I'm driving. I'm following the attorney out to Ted's house. Mr. Ted left me his property and some money to take care of things." *Down here. Away from you and my friends.*

"You're on speaker, right? We don't want to cause an accident." Her mom's worry crossed the network. "Will you be OK seeing Ted's house by yourself?"

"I'll be fine. I just can't believe Ted left me such a

big gift."

"He cared about you, Sam. Who better to inherit than someone young and starting out in life? But I never saw this coming." Sam could almost hear her dad's brain cranking through cost scenarios.

"Yeah, it was a shock to me, too. I'll send pictures when we get there. At least I have a free place to crash while I'm down here."

"Oh, honey. It may not be clean and…" Her mother's overprotective nature bled through the phone lines.

"Mom, Ted had a heart attack at the pharmacy. I'm sure his place is swept clean." Although by her mom's standards, no house was ever perfect. "It's better than a motel. I bet there's even a washer and dryer." She stifled a grin. Her parents meant well, but sometimes they still treated her like a child.

"If you think it's OK?" Her mom was probably processing her daughter's change of plans. A trip to Tennessee wasn't written on the family calendar.

"I'll call you guys later, OK? Love you."

A chorus of 'love you, too' filled her SUV's cabin as she hit the end button. Maybe Ted had the right idea leaving her a new home. She could teach second grade anywhere as long as her certification transferred, or she could continue arranging flowers and wrapping boutonnieres. People in town had to get cancer diagnoses. Though, building a new network of doctors and friends would take time.

Chester's blinker indicated a left turn up ahead. Oak trees towered over the creek that ran parallel to the road. Large branches shaded a bridge crossing the creek.

Once they made it across the bridge, Chester drove to the right and parked on an asphalt clearing near a log house. Her new house. A house with a steepled entry and spindle-railed porch. The ranch home was cute and perfect for an aging teacher, but that teacher wouldn't be coming out the front door and waving a welcome. Her chest squeezed tight over missing the chance to visit Ted here in Whispering Creek. She had promised to see Ted, and then cancer took over her life. *I'm sorry, Mr. Ted.* Under the press of the seatbelt, her breast scar itched.

Grabbing her purse and an accordion file of paperwork, Sam left her coat in the backseat and exited her SUV. The wind nearly swept the car door from her grasp. Her weather app had said chance of rain earlier. With the log house sitting between the creek's oaks and a sea of pine trees across the drive, the wind must have found a breezeway. She clutched her possessions to her side and tried not to shift her plastic breast prosthetic into her armpit. Chester was older, but she was sure he would notice any misalignment.

Chester approached. His brown wingtips scuffed against the blacktop. He gestured toward the wooden-planked porch. "Shall we go inside?" He handed her the keys. Grooves from the metal sawed at her fingertip. The inside of Ted's house could hold more surprises than the deep pockets in her purse.

The rev of an engine drew her attention toward the road. From across the main entrance, a car sped toward where she and Chester had parked. Rubber tires squealed on the asphalt as the driver jammed on the brakes a few feet short of rear-ending Chester's vehicle. A chill shivered down her arms, raising hairs and a warning. How many locals knew she was visiting today?

A salt-and-pepper haired man exited a relic of a station wagon, slammed the door, and marched toward Chester. He resembled Ted, but the stranger was thinner, had a slight stoop, and an untended beard.

She hugged the post of the porch overhang hoping to go unnoticed. This maniac had to be Ernie. What was he planning on doing? Was she about to witness a geriatric beat down? She wrestled with her purse and grabbed her phone. Why couldn't Ernie honor his deceased brother's wishes and Chester's advice? Her finger trembled as she swiped the screen.

A black truck turned into the driveway and pulled in front of her house, parking between her SUV and Chester's vehicle.

Did Ernie bring reinforcements? "Lord, help us," she mumbled.

Why couldn't Chester have handed her a check to fill her bank account? She'd be on the highway north de-stressing like her doctors wanted. She certainly wouldn't be witnessing a countrified cage match.

4

Cole crooned to his bluegrass playlist, drained the last of his soda, and turned onto the private road leading to Ted's log house. To Cole, the oak tree shaded bridge over the creek was a portal into a lazy writing world. An oasis of pine trees surrounded Ted's home instead of the multi-lane freeway that surrounded Nashville. He hoped the retired teacher had gotten his message from the answering machine. Ted's last words in August had been "Come back anytime." Anytime was now, but he didn't want to be an imposition. Cole could almost smell the smoky scent from the firepit he lounged around while Ted's wisdom poured forth. Wisdom that made it into more than one of Cole's songs.

Before he reached Ted's asphalt driveway, a tank of a station wagon passed in front of his truck from the west. He jammed on the brakes as a jolt of adrenaline shot down his back. If he hadn't reacted, the grill of his truck might have catapulted through the old growth oaks and into the creek. The driver couldn't have been Ted. The one-time he and Jillie Lynn had driven with the retired teacher in his white sedan, they had barely broken the speed limit.

Cole turned right and followed the jerk into the

mini parking lot in front of Ted's house. The wannabe racecar driver had stopped and blocked the walkway to the house. Cole parked between two other vehicles facing the shed. Ted had company. Was he hosting a gathering? His friend may have been too busy to call Cole back.

Even from inside his truck, Cole heard the speeding driver berate a man wearing a suit. A young woman stood on the porch by Ted's front door. Was Ted inside calling the sheriff on this crazy? After two hours on the highway listening to steel guitars and country-attitude songs, Cole was ready for a confrontation, especially if Ted was in trouble. He leapt from his truck and shoved his keys in the front pocket of his jeans. Rubbing his fist into his palm, he prepped his muscles and strode toward the commotion.

"This property should have been mine," the driver, a disheveled, gray-haired senior, shouted as he pointed a finger at the pretty lady on the porch. "How dare you bring her here."

The young woman clutched a folder and her purse while thumbing her phone. She was dressed for church not a fist fight.

The older guy in the suit backstepped up the walkway. He eyed Cole suspiciously as Cole drew closer. "Ernie, we talked about this in the office. You need to calm down and go home. I'm implementing Ted's wishes."

"Is there a problem?" Obviously. Cole halted on a strip of grass near the walkway. He propped his hands on his hips. At six-feet-two-inches, he towered over the geriatric crowd.

"Did you call the police?" the scruffy older guy said.

The screamer thought Cole was an off-duty cop. Good. He shrugged in his long-sleeve black t-shirt. Why not play the part and instill some calm and order?

"No, he didn't." The gal on the front porch held her phone high. "But I'm just about to." She ditched her belongings and stomped closer as if she was ready to rumble. The fire in her eyes grew hotter than the red-hot candy he had crunched all the way down I-40. She wasn't a damsel in distress, though Cole wouldn't mind rescuing the spunky stranger.

Cole held up his hands. "I'm not law enforcement. I'm a friend here to see Ted."

Stares and closed lips met his confession. If he knew it was that easy to shut everyone up, he would have stated his business straight away.

Ernie's nose crinkled faster than a potato chip bag. "Well, you're too late. He's dead."

"Dead?" Cole processed the finality of the word. Ted was gone? Ted had called last month to check on him before Jillie Lynn's betrayal. The guy had the biggest heart. Second only to Cole's mom. He scrubbed a hand over his jaw. "I'm sorry to hear that. Real sorry." He nodded. "My condolences." Clearing his throat, he asked, "When did he pass away?"

"A few weeks ago." The professionally dressed man came forward and held out his hand. "I'm Ted's lawyer, Chester Siebold. You're a friend?" The attorney's last question cast doubt on Cole's association. Was he on trial?

"I stayed here last summer. Worked on some…writing." He shook Chester's hand. "Name's Cole Donoven. Ted invited me back. I tried calling, but now I know why my call wasn't returned." Well, so much for stroking his muse. How fast life could change. He knew that from Jillie Lynn's vanishing act.

The gal on the porch strode forward. Her boots clacked on the walkway. "I'm sorry you had to hear about Ted this way. I just found out myself." Her eyelashes fluttered. She rubbed her arm as if she were holding back a crashing wave of tears.

"Don't fall for those crocodile tears," Ernie said. "She stole this house right out from under me. This house should be mine."

"I'm sorry you feel that way, but it is my land now, and you're trespassing." The looker wielded her phone like a sword, aiming the tip at Ernie. "You may leave and come back when you're ready to apologize for your bad manners. I don't accept attitude from my students, and I'm not taking it from a grown man."

Spunky gal had a backbone. Her fiery hazel eyes almost had Cole apologizing for trespassing.

"Sell it to me. How are you going to keep up with this land? I live down the lane." Ernie folded his arms. His mud-covered sneakers weren't moving.

Cole had a vague memory of a relative of Ted's who lived around Whispering Creek. Last time he was here, connecting the dots on a family tree hadn't been a pressing matter.

Gray clouds covered the sky overhead. Maybe rain

would end this awkward stare down.

"You didn't even let us know about the funeral." The lady's lips quivered. "How can I talk about selling this property when I haven't even been inside the home he wanted me to have?"

"I have," Cole answered. Everyone turned his direction as if he were a pesky horsefly. "Been inside." He swallowed hard. Emotional women were one of his weaknesses. He stretched his back and cracked a few knuckles. "I'll show you around." He captured the watery gaze of Ted's heiress. "After Ernie leaves."

Ernie blanched and turned toward the attorney. "This buck could be a burglar or a murderer. What if he's telling us lies?"

The heiress barked out a laugh. "That's one way you could get my land. The ink on the papers may not be dry."

Cole laughed at the girl's wit. When her eyebrow shot up giving him a conspiratorial, tell-me-you're-not-a-murderer look, his chest rumbled a few more chuckles. Man, it felt good to enjoy life for a moment. He held up his hands as if he was under arrest. "I've never killed anyone nor stolen property. I have told a few white lies, but staying with Ted isn't one of them." He winked at Ernie.

"Wait." Chester wagged a manicured finger in Cole's direction. "I think I met you last summer in town at the coffee shop. You were with that girl."

"That girl" was one way to describe a country starlet whose curves could stop traffic. Cole grinned and rubbed his smooth-shaven jaw. "It's funny how people remember her and forget about me."

"Well, I'm not forgetting about you." Ted's heiress waved for him to follow her. "Please, come inside." Her chin tilted toward the sky as she glanced at the clouds above.

He stepped between the two older gentlemen. "It's been nice meeting you." Was that a white lie? "I am sorry for your loss. Ted was a great guy. He was my friend." Truth in abundance. He nodded at Chester and Ernie before following his hostess to the door. Whatever perfume she was wearing reminded him of flowery soap. The scent kept his boots shuffling after her shiny, shoulder-length hair.

"Deal with me next time, Ernie," Chester scolded. "Let me handle the estate." Finally, the attorney was running interference.

The girl reclaimed file folders and opened the front door. "Whatever happened to Southern hospitality? I can't believe Ernie and Ted were raised by the same mother. In all the years I knew Ted, I don't think I ever heard him raise his voice." She stopped on the threshold. "Wait."

Was she changing her mind about inviting him in? He halted a few feet from the door.

"I promised Emma and my parents that I would take a picture of the house. Will you stand by the door?"

"Does your friend Emma have facial-recognition software?" He waggled his eyebrows to make her laugh again. He liked her laugh, and he hoped she didn't send him packing right away. He shoved his hands into his pockets and grinned like a long-lost cousin.

She stood at the edge of the porch, held up her phone, and snapped a picture. "I'm not sure about facial recognition, but if I give her your name, she'll stalk you on social media."

"Cole Donoven, with an e. She'll hit on Donoven and Son Electric in Nashville. Don't hold my picture against me. My Dad and my older brother update their pictures on the website regularly. Mine hasn't been updated in like ten years." No one in his former company seemed to mind he looked like a teenager.

"You are brave giving me all that information, Cole Donoven, with an e." She swept her arm toward the foyer. "Come on in. Especially if you give house tours and discounts on electrical work. I hope you know what a God-send you are. I thought I was going to have to call 911, and I don't even know my address."

He'd do her electrical work for free. This girl was a balm for his spirit. He scraped his cowboy boots on the planked porch to remove any dirt. "Is your friend Emma in Wisconsin?"

She stiffened and turned his direction, brushing a strand of light brown hair behind her ear. "How did you know that? By my accent?"

Laughter rumbled in his chest again. Accent? Who was she kidding? She hadn't drawled a single word. "There's a car sitting out front with Wisconsin plates." He hooked a thumb toward the drive. "I may not be a cop, but your attorney talks like me. I figure he's driving the luxury vehicle with the court doctor plates."

Through the large front window, he watched Ernie speeding away, the man's thin frame hunched over the wheel.

"You could be a detective." She looked around, taking in the sitting area and the kitchen table. She blew out a breath. "I can picture Ted in this house. He didn't like to throw things away that were still sturdy." Her voice deepened on the last two words. "This gold couch is an antique," she mimicked Ted's confidant voice. Her smile quivered. "I remember it from grade school. And Nan's rocker. I can still picture her reading me a book in it." Tears welled in her eyes. "Ted's death has turned my life upside down."

"I know how you feel." And he did. He didn't recognize the life he had been living since Jillie Lynn wrapped herself in someone else's sheets. "I'm so sorry about, Ted, uh…"

"Oh." Her lips formed a perfect little O. She held out her hand. "I'm Samantha, but everyone calls me Sam."

He grasped her soft, warm hand. He was sorry Ted had passed away. He truly was, but Ted's passing had brought this Yankee in her form-fitting dress to his backyard. Conversing with her was like talking to a friend who lived down the block. For the first time since Jillie Lynn left, Cole didn't feel like isolating from the world.

The lawyer darted into the house. "It's starting to rain."

Cole released Sam's hand as a tear snaked down

her cheek. Water was dripping inside and outside Ted's house. Too bad he couldn't hang around Wisconsin Sam for a week and see what her muse might whisper.

5

After placing her belongings on the kitchen counter, Sam clutched her phone to her chest. Her mind raced back in time when she would curl up in Nan's lap and her neighbor would read their favorite detective stories. Ted would lounge on the gilded couch scanning the newspaper and commenting on the cliffhanger endings to the novel's chapters. *What do you think happens next, Sammy?* Strange how the human brain could replay Ted's voice as if he were standing beside her. Sam expected the aroma of fresh baked shortbread cookies to waft from the spotless kitchen. Dang cancer. She should have visited Ted here in Whispering Creek. Now she was hanging around his empty house and contemplating its sale.

"Excuse me, but I need to use the bathroom. Been on the road for a couple hours." Cole gave commentary as he went down the hall. "There's a half-bath off the kitchen, a full bath in the master bedroom, and another in the hallway." Not only did Cole scare off disgruntled neighbors, he also knew the layout of her house. Cole was like her real estate angel with his helpful spirit. The guy must have had Ted's seal of approval since Ted invited Cole to stay with him. If only she could forget her attorney's delight at the mention of some girl.

Chester surveyed the living area. "Shall we take a look around and make sure everything is in order before I leave? It doesn't look as if anyone has been in here since Ted's death."

She was thankful for small miracles.

Her phone vibrated as she followed Chester through the living room and toward the hall.

Nice house. Who's the hottie? Emma texted a flame for emphasis.

How did she explain Cole to Emma? He wasn't technically a neighbor or a friend.

Friend of Ted's. Cole Donoven. Father owns an electrical company.

If he has a black cowboy hat, I'm so there.

Sam grinned and let her friend's enthusiasm for Ted's house and its former guest encourage her soul. *Don't know about the Stetson. I'll check (:*

Cole was nice looking without a Stetson. He must have a good heart too, or Ted would have kicked him out the door.

Another notification lit up her phone.

Her mom texted. *The house is adorable. Ted's atty looks so young. Is he a paralegal? When will u be back? Call us tonight.* Several hearts followed her mom's text.

I'll call later. Taking a tour with atty. Which she should begin.

Cole's bootsteps echoed on the wood floor in the hallway. "Haven't gotten too far on your tour."

"Haven't really started." She peeked in Ted's bedroom. Cole joined her while Chester glanced out the bedroom window.

The navy bedspread was military inspection perfect. A picture of Nan graced the dresser and so did a photograph of a young Sam pumping her legs on a tree swing. She fanned her face with her hand warning her tears to stay put. *I'll see you in heaven, Nan and Ted.* What a comfort she had to ease her grief.

Cole and Chester escorted her down the hallway. Pictures from Nan and Ted's wedding and their fiftieth anniversary party decorated the wall. She glanced in the other two bedrooms and followed the men through the laundry room into the kitchen. She flipped on all the kitchen lights to combat the nasty gray sky outside. As she turned on the light above the stainless-steel sink, the entire kitchen went dark.

"What's wrong with the lights?" Not the best way to start her home ownership.

"Maybe it's the circuit breaker." Chester checked his watch. He didn't move his wingtips toward the breaker box.

"It's not a bad breaker. Although some shops would charge you to add one. I told Ted to go with LEDs. They pull less wattage and don't overload the circuit." Cole had the light on his phone illuminating the laundry room tile. "I bought some bulbs for Ted the last time I was here. He wasn't a fan of the shape, and it looks like he never switched them out. It's an easy fix to lower the wattage." Cole reached above the washing machine and opened a cupboard. "Found 'em." He turned her direction. "You don't mind me swapping them out, do you?"

"Sure. That'd be great." She had no idea what he was talking about, but if he could get the lights working, she would give him a smiley sticker. Cole probably thought she was useless. She wasn't an airhead when it came to home repair, but she should have spent more time with her dad when he was fixing things around the house. Karlton wasn't handy. Her ex didn't know his way around a screwdriver unless it contained orange juice.

Chester cleared his throat. "Do you mind if I head out? The house is in good shape, and Ernie hasn't returned to cause any trouble. I'd like to get on the road before it pours." He tilted his gray hair ever so slightly toward Cole whose attention was enraptured with an LED bulb and a hard to reach socket. "That is, if you're comfortable."

"Of course." Why shouldn't she be? Ted was a good judge of character. Emma probably had Cole's bio and last known address plugged into the note app on her phone. Besides, Chester could identify Cole in a line up. "Thank you for showing me the house and handling all of the paperwork."

"I'll call you Monday about the filings." Chester shook her hand. "Good afternoon, Mr. Donoven."

Cole waved a hand from atop the counter. "Nice meeting you. I'll have the lights back on for your client in no time."

Her attorney nodded and hurried out the door.

Sam sauntered over by Cole and took the wrapping off the last box of bulbs. She'd make a note what to buy for next time.

"Thanks for fixing the lighting. I'm used to wrestling a dozen thorned roses or breaking up two boys in a recess kicking match."

"Life is rough in Wisconsin." He grinned as if he was a second-grade boy about to get into mischief.

She laughed as heat swept from her neck into her cheeks. Emma was correct. Cole was handsome, cowboy hat or not. "My teaching degree didn't come with electrical skills."

"What are friends for? If you think of me as a friend." He ran a hand through his wavy dark hair. "I'd rather screw in a bulb than wrangle kids all day." He hopped off the counter. "I'll use a chair to reach the ceiling fixture, and then we should be good."

Would she be good? Strolling into the living room, she stared out the picture window. All the memories she had made with Nan and Ted threatened to overrun her mind and burst her heart. The ache consumed her chest and made her want to sit in Nan's rocker and cry. The clouds outside were as gloomy as her mood. Stupid cancer kept her from seeing Ted's new home and hugging him one last time.

Her one ray of sunshine was her new friend Cole. He had saved her twice today. Once with Ernie and once with her wattage issue. When his work order was complete, he would leave, and she would be alone with her inheritance.

The kitchen lights clicked to life, brightening the foyer.

Cole crossed his arms and tapped his cowboy boot on the floor. "We are back in business."

A weird howl sounded in the distance. It reminded her of a lonely coyote on a December night or a low, far off engine whistle.

"Are there train tracks around here?" She strode toward Cole and her cheery kitchen.

Cole cocked his head. A loud screech emanated from his pocket. His brow furrowed as he pulled out his phone.

She covered her ears. Unease swirled in her belly. "What is going on?"

Eyes wide, he said, "Tornado."

Mind a jumble, she shouted, "Where's the basement?"

"There isn't one."

Before she could lament her deteriorating life, Cole swept her in his arms. Her face smashed against his firm chest as he raced through the laundry room, down the hall, and almost dropped her in the bathtub before he dove onto the floor. A loud thud echoed from the roof. She squeezed her hands into fists and curled tight against the cold porcelain. The shattering of glass interrupted the wind. *Lord, protect us.*

Lights in the hall went dark.

"I can't believe this is happening." She could barely process all the changes coming her way.

"Stay low, Sam." Cole's rugged voice sounded an octave higher.

How much lower could her life get? Ted's house, no her house, might blow away with her and her new friend in it. And she wasn't even confident she had insurance.

6

Cole sprawled on the bathroom floor facing the tub. How long did one wait for a tornado to end? He would have sworn he'd been waiting a week for the creaks and howls to cease, but with a glance at his phone, it had only been twenty minutes. So far, his relaxing weekend had turned into a wild carnival ride. His adrenaline rush was still waning from his mad dash from the kitchen. All he had focused on was getting Sam to safety. He hadn't penned one line in a new song, but God was giving him lots of material to use.

Whispers and mumbled words carried over the tub. Was Sam praying? Maybe he should utter a prayer of thanks that they were still alive. *Thank You, Lord.* Short and sweet.

"Do you think it's over?" Sam's head popped over the tub wall. Static electricity had her hair flying high. He wanted to laugh, but hurting her feelings wasn't cool. Something, perhaps fleeing a killer whirlwind with her in his arms had him hoping he could get to know her better. He had been in her presence less than an hour, yet she had boosted his ego ten times above normal. His ex-girlfriend had dismissed his apprenticeship in the trades. Sam appreciated his skill and handiwork with the lightbulbs.

"It's pretty quiet. Let me take a look outside." He rose and lifted the blinds on the bathroom window. "The rain's stopped. Some of the trees near the creek are pretty beat up and have lost branches. Good news, the gray clouds are moving south." Better news, the alarm from his phone had given them time to get to safety.

Sam brushed hair out of her face and stood. She clutched her phone like it was a treasure. "I heard glass breaking." Her forehead creased as she bit her lip.

"Me, too." He helped her step out of the tub. No killer-tipped fingernails poked his palm. Her sparkly nails were short and practical. "Let me check the hall."

He eased the door open in case the bathroom was the only room left standing. Peeking into the hallway, he didn't notice any damage. "Looks OK from here. I don't know about the front rooms."

"Lead the way. I've only owned this home for hours, and now it might need major repairs." Her mouth pulled downward as she rotated her right shoulder.

"Might is the key word." Enough rain had fallen on her home inspection. He indicated her shoulder. "Did I hurt you?"

Her eyes grew wide as she shook her head. "It's been a while since I've been in a tub. No rubber duckies for me."

She followed him into the living room, halted, and threaded fingers through her hair. The window near the golden sofa had been smashed by a leafy oak. The pane had broken out in large pieces with a few splinters.

"Oh, no." Sam's shoulders slumped. She blew out a long breath as she surveyed the damage. "I'll have to call Chester and find out who I call about this mess." She shifted the sofa away from the wet leaves while he helped move the table and Nan's rocker. "Do you think Chester made it home before the storm? Otherwise, I'll need housewarming gifts from Glass Repairs Are Us."

Her sense of humor was better than a swig from an energy drink. "At least the roof's intact. We can remove the large panes of glass and cover the opening. The porch railing might need some repair." He sympathized with her. No matter how off course his weekend had gotten, hers was definitely worse.

He opened the front door to a waft of freshly tilled earth and halted on the porch. Sam's misfortune must have rubbed off on him during their rush to safety. A long object had impaled his truck's passenger side window and decided to take out his windshield as well. His front wheel well curled inward. No plunger was taking out that dent.

Turning toward Sam, he pointed to his pickup. "Looks like I spoke too soon about shattered glass." He'd have to call a glass service before he could head back to Nashville. Storm damage would keep him in Whispering Creek for at least another day. If his truck wasn't drivable, it would be longer.

He tilted his head toward the sky. The last of the ominous clouds were hightailing it out of his sight. He didn't mind spending more time with Sam, but he would have preferred to get to know her at a nice restaurant, driving in a pristine truck. Guess he should make the best of what God gave him. Hadn't he and Sam been praying moments ago?

"Whoa." Sam came alongside him on the edge of the porch. "Whatever came through here didn't like your truck." She picked up a branch from the felled tree that had broken the front window. A sea of leaves littered the plank porch along with a few shingles. "I am so, so sorry."

"I think my culprit is the guard rail from the bridge." He headed to inspect the crumpled steel above his deflating tire. His boots crunched on the pebbles and twigs peppered on the damp asphalt. So far, only one wheel had been hit.

Sam hopped over a puddle as she walked past his truck. "If it's any consolation. I think your truck spared my car." She continued down the drive dodging tree limbs and debris. She stopped and placed a hand on her shapely hip. "I don't think either of us is traveling over the creek today. The storm uprooted a large oak. It's blocking the main drive and some of Ernie's lane."

Make that a two-day stay in Whispering Creek. It was already Saturday afternoon, and he doubted crews would clear debris on Sunday. *God, You sure have a way of turning a guy's life upside down.*

"Do you think we should check on Ernie?" Sam nibbled her lip. "He is my neighbor and Ted's brother. What if something fell on him or his wife?"

Such a teacher comment. He pictured her breaking up a fight in her classroom and making the kids apologize. His conscience pinged. His mother would show the same compassion. Mom was the first to bring someone a meal after an injury or illness. She would like Sam.

Funny too, how practical and calm Sam was being with the chaos. Jillie Lynn would be freaking out about now and screaming at someone to fix the problem. Calm was nice. He hadn't experienced calm in two years.

Sam cocked her head and gave him a you-know-I'm-right look. "Do unto others, Cole."

"I guess. Sure." Way to impress her with his Christian values. The ones he hadn't been living of late. Sam still stared at him with her mesmerizing eyes. Teacher hypnosis.

"OK. I'll be a Good Samaritan. Walk a lady across the road. Keep Ernie alive so he can scream at us another day." If he stayed for a few days, he might as well be neighborly and earn points with Sam. He hoped Ernie didn't chase off do-gooders with a gun.

Sam headed toward her SUV. "Are we walking over? I've got some hiking boots in my car."

He didn't remember exactly how far down the lane the other house was located. He had seen it from the all-terrain vehicle trails last summer but wasn't paying much attention. The old guy didn't traipse over on foot either.

Cole jogged to the shed. A couple of pine trees had been uprooted and rested against the side wall. He silently thanked the Lord that Sam didn't have more storm damage.

"Ted had a gator in the shed. If it's still here, we can ride over to Ernie's."

"Gator?" Sam called from the backseat of her SUV while she laced her boots.

"It's like a monster golf cart on steroids. A utility vehicle. Ted let me drive it on some trails in the hills last summer." Those were some fun times. If only he'd come back sooner. He owed Ted his gratitude for giving him fond memories and enough songs to keep Slater off his back. Off his back until now. Leave it to Jillie Lynn to choose a relentless manager and then to bolt, leaving Cole to uphold the overzealous commitment.

Sam slammed the car door and approached the shed looking as if she was about to march to church or school. "If you remember the code, I'll be impressed."

"Remembering 1234 isn't impressive." He laughed as the whirr of the rising door broke the peaceful silence after the storm. Dust particles danced in the wake of the retreating door. Sure enough. Ted had a ride that wasn't full of splintered glass. Cole sauntered alongside the utility vehicle and surveyed Ted's power tools. "There may even be a chain saw we can use to clear Ernie's lane."

Her boisterous laughter rang out as she entered the shade of the shed. "I've taught a lesson on stranger danger, and I'm pretty sure driving with an almost stranger into the wilderness when he's carrying a chain saw wouldn't pass my test. I'm putting an awful lot of trust in you, Cole Donoven with an e."

Bottling that fun laugh and putting it in a song

would earn him a spot at number one on the country charts. He rolled his shoulders and broadened his chest. "It's my policeman vibe. People let their guard down and invite me into their home." He grinned as she shook her light brown hair. She was cute even in hiking boots and a dress. "Trust me. You can see Ernie's house if we go high enough into the hills. I figure if we head in the right direction, we'll end up where we want to be."

Sam cocked her head. "Ya know, that last line sounds like a country song." She hopped into the passenger seat of the utility vehicle. "I might use it in my prayers tonight."

He thought back over his words and grinned. Whispering Creek was living up to its reputation. "Sounds like we have a similar prayer request." And he had one line of a song that his new friend and muse thought was wise and prayer worthy. He slid into the driver's seat ready for their next adventure.

7

Sam held tight to the hand grip in the gator as Cole drove the utility vehicle up a sloping hill and banked left through a row of evergreens. The uneven ground and the fast speed caused her backside to absorb a few bumps. She'd tolerate the assault on her bones to make sure Ted's brother and his wife were safe, but she wouldn't be volunteering to ride in the passenger seat again soon. Spreading some of Ted's generosity was the least she could do after all the kindness he'd shown her during her twenty-three years.

"Heads up," Cole said before another dip jostled the gator.

Her shoulder brushed against Cole's arm. The same strong arm that carried her away from the storm and toward safety in the bathroom. The feel of his broad chest replayed pleasantly in her mind as a faint hint of his earthy cologne clung to her dress. Her thoughts sobered. Had Cole felt her prosthetic during his race down the hallway? How would he have reacted to her diagnosis? Karlton's affection waned after her implant failed, and she had moved in with her parents.

Her grip tightened on the plastic handle to the side

of the passenger seat as Cole maneuvered the tree line. With all the bumps, the soft plastic prosthetic shifted in her bra. She had to stop thinking about her loss and her lost relationship. Being alive was better than being pine-boxed in a cancer grave. God had given her new days to celebrate.

Stay focused on the present. She swallowed sour saliva and concentrated on being a helpful neighbor. She also made a mental note of what she would do first if Ernie's house was a pile of pick-up sticks. Call 911 for a chopper. Search for Ernie and his wife in the rubble. Begin CPR.

Cole rounded a spindly-branched fir, and Ernie's home came into view. The ranch home rivaled the size of Ted's but had a smaller porch and faded white siding instead of a log facade. A few shingles were missing, and a gutter dangled out of place. The storm hadn't shattered glass or destroyed Ernie's cars.

Her elderly neighbor stood on a strip of grass in front of his porch. A navy-colored baseball cap shielded his eyes. Ernie turned toward the sound of the rumbling UTV. His mouth gaped and then pressed tight in a not-you-again challenge.

She hoped being a good neighbor would be rewarded with a kind greeting and not screams or accusations.

Cole slowed the gator and parked near the porch. He shut off the engine, leaving an eerie quiet. Stroking his chin, he gave her a sly wink as if they had a secret plan to execute.

"Here comes the sheriff," Ernie muttered. He

embedded his hands on his hips and mumbled something about the gator. His attitude had survived intact. "What are you doing here?" Ernie shuffled away from the grass and the utility vehicle and toward a sedan resting next to the faded brown station wagon that had terrorized them earlier. The old man pointed at the white sedan. "Don't go saying anything about the car. Ted left it to me fair and square."

High winds hadn't tempered Ernie's spunk. Sam held her hands in surrender mode. She wouldn't haggle over something she didn't need or want. "I have a vehicle. My SUV is running fine. We came to make sure you were safe from the storm."

Cole exited the vehicle through the non-existent door and surveyed the roof of Ernie's house. "We wanted to make sure you were OK. We had some damage and thought the storm may have struck here first. I see some of your shingles are gone. I think they may be over at Ted's place."

Sam released her grip and opened her hand as a slight ache pulsed through her knuckles. Thankfully, Cole had referred to her property as Ted's home. She slipped off the hard plastic seat and strode toward the men.

"So, are you going to keep my shingles, too?" Ernie pushed his cap back on his head releasing a mat of gray hair. "I came out to see about those trees." He swung his hat in the direction of the blocked asphalt drive. "We're unharmed, but we're stuck here. There's no way I'm driving my cars through the rutted dirt or through the creek." Ernie voice emboldened, emphasizing his ownership of the vehicles.

With Ernie's older and frail bone structure, he could break a hip on some of the bumps she'd endured.

She stifled a grin and shaded her eyes to assess the size of the branches. "We brought a chain saw. I'm no help, but Cole knows how to use it." At least she hoped he did. He had loaded it in the gator with gasoline and gloves as if he was making a home improvement commercial.

~*~

An older woman hobbled out the front door and onto the porch. She grasped the railing and steadied herself. A black medical boot covered one foot and ankle.

"Ernest, stop harassing those kids. There is no way you and I are clearing that drive." The lady's voice had a queen-of-the-castle air. She bestowed a grandmotherly smile upon them. The woman's presence had cut the tension like a switchblade. "You probably don't remember me, Sam, but I'm Ernie's wife, Gretta. You sure have grown since I saw you last."

Truth be told, Sam wouldn't have recognized Gretta in a line up if her life depended on it. It had to have been fifteen years since she had last laid eyes on Ernie and his wife. "Nice to see you again, Gretta."

Sam walked to the bottom of the porch steps and indicated Cole. "This is a friend of Ted's. Cole

Donoven." Should she have introduced Cole as her friend? After all they had been through together, Cole was more than an acquaintance. Though, when the drive was cleared and his truck was fixed, he'd drive off and become a "Like" on social media. Too bad there wasn't a replica of Cole in Wisconsin.

"Nice to meet you, ma'am." Cole waved. "You've got some damage to your shingles. Do you have any water dripping through?"

Could Cole fix roofs as well as do electrical work?

"Don't sweet talk my wife." Ernie traipsed toward the porch steps. "I'm not finished with that attorney yet."

"Oh, yes, you are." Gretta pulled the sides of her pink cardigan together. "We'd appreciate your help. I called the electric company, and no one is coming until things are settled in town. Most of the homes are without power from the microburst." She propped her black boot on the edge of the porch step. "I'm useless with this torn Achilles' tendon."

It would have been nice to have Gretta's civility earlier. Ernie must have sneaked out of the house or outrun her to the door.

"We're glad you're not hurt from the storm. We were worried." Sam rubbed her arm and leaned against the porch railing. She wasn't cold. December in Tennessee was balmy in her book. The caress of her arm was what her mother would do to calm Sam's worries, or help Sam solve a problem. One item was scratched off her worry list. Ernie and Gretta were alive, and one was cantankerous.

Now they had to clear what they could off the driveway and hope electrical crews came soon. If they didn't, what would she do with Cole after dark?

Cole joined their soirèe at the porch steps. "I've got Ted's chainsaw and some goggles and gloves." He hitched his thumb toward the back of the gator. "We should be able to get most of your lane cleared." *We?* A glorious we. Thank goodness Cole didn't know about her cancer surgeries, or she might be relegated to the porch chairs with Gretta. Her family had a hard time believing she was healthy.

Squinting toward where the main entrance to the properties laid, Cole said, "There's a mammoth tree covering the bridge over the creek. Some of the debris damaged my truck. There's no telling when we'll get electricity back if branches took out the power lines."

Ernie replaced his baseball cap and rubbed the bill up and down on his forehead. "You two going to do all this work?" He cast a glance at the hem of her dress. "I've got a wheelbarrow for transporting the wood."

Sam backstepped toward Cole. "He'll cut, and I'll drag and stack. You can show me where to pile the wood or help drive the wheelbarrow." Supervising the work should make Ernie happy. She was thrilled that no one had a gaped-mouth, panicked look about a former cancer patient helping with the labor.

"I've got aprons for you both. It'll keep the dirt off." Gretta rotated slowly toward the door.

Cole clapped his hands and rubbed them together. "Only for Sam. Loose clothing isn't good around vibrating blades."

With as slow as Gretta moved, receiving the apron might take an hour of daylight. Sam stepped toward the older woman.

Gretta blocked Sam's ascent with a pink-sweatered arm. "I can manage. Ernest can bring the apron out to you. And when you're finished, don't race off. I managed to bake cookies this morning before the power failed. We'll pack a plate for you. I might have an extra pack of hot dogs, too. Some of the food at Ted's has to be spoiled."

Sam's stomach gurgled at the mention of cookies. "Thank you. I hadn't even thought about cleaning out the fridge. That's another task for my to-do list."

Cole came alongside her as Ernie dutifully followed his wife inside. "Man, if I knew she had cookies, I would have raced over here straightaway."

"We did come over pretty fast."

"After you talked some sense into me." Cole headed to the back of their vehicle.

"Oh, come on, Sheriff. You would have moseyed over sooner or later."

A pair of gloves sailed her direction. She caught them before they hit the dirt.

Ernie's squeaking sneakers sounded against the porch planks.

"Here you go." Ernie held out an apron. He rocked on his feet as if he was ready to bolt.

Sam slipped the apron over her head and tied it in the back. Her protective layer said Grandma Bakes.

"Come on, Granny." Cole mimicked an aged man, humped over, with a steadying hand on his hip. "We have work to do." His fake falsetto voice trailed off as he hefted the chain saw and a gas can from the back of the gator. "Ready?" He lifted his brows and flashed a serious expression as if they were setting off on a military mission. But it was the gleam of delight in his eyes that provoked a smile from her. Cole was having fun. Of course, what guy wouldn't want to drive a four-wheeler, wield a chain saw, and eat cookies? Even with all the chaos, in this moment, gazing into Cole's dark brown eyes, she was having fun, too.

Eight months ago, after recovering from her second surgery, she might have walked slow like a granny, but not now, not after healing and being declared cancer-free. "Ready when you are, Sheriff." She marched down the puddled lane toward the felled oak with a renewed vigor in her steps. The air smelled like the lumber aisle at the local home improvement store. "Chainsaw away."

"Kids," Ernie remarked, traipsing to the back of the house.

Cole cut off the thinner, leafy branches, and Sam dragged them into the brush by the creek that ran between the road and Ernie and Ted's land. She hadn't heard any creek noise prior to the storm, but now God had turned on a spigot and the gurgling rush of water was audible. She stacked the thicker, firewood length logs on the side of Ernie's house. Ted's brother didn't complain when he showed her the pebbled area where he already had some wood piled. Ernie even made a few trips back and forth with the wheelbarrow which saved her arms. She prayed that completing this task together would soften Ernie's gruff manner.

After about an hour of transporting tree limbs off the drive, she turned to go and pile Cole's latest chunks of wood in the wheelbarrow. Her partner in cleanup silenced the chainsaw.

Mr. Lumberjack removed his black shirt. Sam's mouth dried like the Sahara at the sight of Cole's tanned and defined muscles battling the oak. Whew! Tennessee was getting hotter.

"Lemonade," Gretta called from the porch.

Could she bathe in it? Sam's gaze needed a cold splash. *Lord, what am I doing here so far from home drooling over the guy you stranded me with?* What were those Bible verses about lust? She remembered a song they sang in Sunday school. "Be 'Careful Little Eyes.'" She definitely couldn't unsee this sight. Yet, enjoying the view of Cole's muscled chest clenched her heart. Her own chest was uneven and scarred. With a prosthetic, she deceived everyone. She joked that her plastic breast was false advertising, but the joke was on her. She prayed that in time the uneasiness would go away, or at least the fear of another attempt at reconstructive surgery would flee.

"It's a good time for a break." Cole swiped sweat from his brow. "We've cleared a nice pathway. I'll be there in a minute. I need to cool down a bit."

Sam joined Gretta and Ernie on the porch and sat in an Adirondack chair next to her hostess. Flecks of bark decorated the sleeves of Sam's dress beyond the protection of her apron. No doubt she smelled like a person who was ignorant of deodorant.

Ernie excused himself and went inside the house. His baseball cap rested on the small round table next to Gretta.

Gretta leaned in close. Her blue-eyed gaze flickered to where Ernie had departed. "I'd offer for you to stay to dinner, but well, Ernest likes his privacy. Maybe after all this estate stuff settles down, I'll have you over. Tonight, Ernest will have to heat something over the firepit for us."

"I understand." Sam sipped her lemonade and allowed the sweet citrus taste to energize her mouth. Would she still be here after the estate settled? She wasn't sure of the fate of Ted's house. "I'll be around for a few more days. My stay here in Whispering Creek is being extended thanks to the weather."

That conspiratorial gleam in Gretta's eyes remained. "Well, Mother Nature's gentler side didn't leave you stranded alone." The older woman smiled, her coral lipstick contrasting with her alabaster skin. "Your Cole is a sweetheart helping us after the storm. You've always been a sweetheart." Gretta grasped Sam's hand. The older woman's skin was cool, yet soft and comforting.

Your Cole. Cole wasn't hers, not in the way Gretta insinuated.

She squeezed Gretta's hand and thanked the Lord silently that she and Cole had come to check on the neighbors. Her neighbors, for the time being.

Sitting low to the ground in her porch chair, with Gretta's baby powder scent wafting on the breeze, Sam rejoiced that she could be the wood-toting rescuer for a moment in time. She didn't have a radiation rash, or infection, or a fever. The overprotective, but well-meaning pampering of her parents remained hundreds of miles away. She relished the slight ache in her muscles and the glimpse of the life she used to live when all she thought about were lesson plans and weekend plans with friends. Her simpler, healthier, independent life.

Cole sauntered toward the porch. He pulled his black tee over his head and covered his abs.

When darkness came, she had to figure out what to do with her newfound friend. Though, one rule would be set in stone. Cole Donoven had to keep his shirt on. Rugged, good-hearted men were a temptation in the moonlight.

Hmm. She gathered her hair, grabbed an elastic from her pocket, and secured the strands in a ponytail. Why were her thoughts starting to sound like song lyrics?

8

Foot on the gas pedal, Cole drove the gator down the edge of the asphalt drive toward Ted's house. Now that Ernie and Gretta were set right, he'd see to the damage he and Sam had left behind. Even after cutting wood for over an hour, he was revved. Being outdoors in the fresh air and warm sunshine with a pretty woman made him hyper as a high schooler on spring break. Whispering Creek was making life fun again. He had to start writing some of the craziness into a song.

"Are we going to ration those cookies?" He nodded at the plate Sam had cradled in her lap. She didn't death grip the hand hold for stability on the smooth asphalt drive home.

"Cookies, no. Hot dogs, yes. I haven't eaten anything since breakfast, and I'm famished. I think these might be Nan's Christmas cookie recipe. They don't have frosting, though."

"Look pretty boring to me, but I'm not complaining." He parked the utility vehicle by the porch and lifted the plastic wrap on the cookies enough to steal one from her lap. After his first swallow, he said, "Yep, boring." A few birds sing-songed his assessment.

"Sugar cookies are supposed to be plain." She gave him a get-with-the-program look. "Decorations make them fun."

"How about we throw in some red hots? I have some in my truck. We'll make them Nashville hot." His candy was probably covered in glass shards, but he couldn't stop teasing the teacher about her bland cookies.

"No way. You're not ruining my meal." She turned toward the driver's seat, carefully holding Gretta's gifts. "I'll set these inside while we clean up the glass. I want to wash my hands."

Cole pocketed the gator's keys and leaned back against the stiff seat. "Ted is on well water. If the power's out, there's no electricity for the pump."

Sam sighed and sputtered. "Great. No power. No water. What's next? Oh, wait." Her eyes brightened. "I have water in my trunk. I've already winterized my car."

He laughed at her change in mood. Frustration to elation in a millisecond. And he might be stepping in his own ignorance, but he had to ask. "You winterize your car with bottled water?"

She nodded with attitude. Here came some northern wisdom.

"You don't want to get stuck somewhere when it's twenty below. I've got water, a blanket, ice scraper, salt, and jumper cables in my trunk." Her eyes widened. "And granola bars. There's our breakfast." She briefly pointed a finger at him, all the while protecting her plated stash of food.

"Life's tough up north. Guess I'd be a goner. Or a popsicle." He stroked his jaw and hid his grin. "I think your water would turn into a popsicle in twenty below, too."

Her mouth blew out a gust almost as loud as the storm.

He'd corrected the teacher. Why was it so much fun bantering with her?

A notification sounded from her purse on the floor of the passenger seat. *Saved by the bell.* Sam bent over and scrounged for her phone.

She hunched in the seat and checked her messages. "Uh oh. My mom's been trying to get a hold of me. Her last text sounds frantic. I'd better give her a call." With her hair tucked behind her ear, he could see her furrowed brow become smooth as silk. "Looks like my attorney's alive though. Chester wants me to check in. Apparently, he had pulled off the road and was lying in a ditch when I tried to contact him earlier."

"It's good to know there's still one more attorney in the world." He chuckled at his joke.

Sam laughed as she shifted in her seat and got out of the gator, balancing the package of hot dogs on top of the cookies.

Cole exited the driver's seat, rested an arm on top of the vehicle's roof, and faced Sam. "I'll bring some garbage cans from the shed so we have a place to put all our debris."

"This sure isn't how I thought my time in Whispering Creek would go." She adjusted her purse on her shoulder. "I'd better make my calls, and then I'll clear the living room of glass." She rounded the gator's camouflaged hood just as the ding of another message sounded through the leather of her purse.

"Not again." She bit her lip while casting a glance his direction. "My parents have been overprotective lately. I moved in with them last spring after a health emergency. They don't always badger me, but it was easier to live with them after I had surgery." She shrugged and shook her hair as if she were forgetting rain clouds from the past. "My mom's a nurse, and well, why pay rent when you're on leave from teaching and you can have a nurse at your fingertips." Her former perky vibe returned. "I'm surprised your parents haven't called." She gave him a side-eyed glance he wouldn't mind receiving after a beer in the moonlight. "Or that girl."

Thrumming his fingers on the gator's roof, he let the statement that actually seemed a question hang in the humid air between them before answering. Sam must have heard Chester's remark when the attorney remembered meeting Jillie Lynn in town. He tamped his joy that Sam was curious about his relationship status. Why else bring up his girlfriend? His lip twitched as he controlled his glee.

"My folks live in Nashville. Our storm was traveling the opposite direction. They probably think I'm lounging on my couch watching college football." If his dad even cared. His brother handled the business's emergency calls on Saturdays.

"They don't know you came out here?"

"Nope." He swaggered a few steps closer and

crossed his arms over his chest. Good. His shirt was almost dry. He tipped forward on his booted toes. "And that girl, Jillie Lynn, is out of the picture."

"Oh." She grew a bit taller. Her eyelashes fluttered as though she were processing the news. Then her posture relaxed. "Oh, Cole." Her voice cooed his name as if she were apologizing for Jillie Lynn's disappearing act. "I'm sorry about Jillian. I shouldn't have said anything. I was just…"

"It's Jillie Lynn."

"What?" Sam didn't move. She could have been a wax figurine until she sucked in her lip and a tiny grunt rumbled in her throat. Her chest started jiggling. "I'm so sorry, Jim Bob." She tried to cover her laughter. No use. The girl was in full giggle mode.

"I know a few people with two names." He settled his hands on his hips. "Makes a kid stand out."

A bit of decorum followed. "I am sorry…about Silly Jillie." The laughter was back. Sam held the package of franks against her mouth to quiet the outburst. "It's…" More wiener-muted chuckling. "I've never heard that name before."

He wished he hadn't heard it either. The betrayal wasn't fully scabbed over. Cole had quit his dad's company to write songs with JL. He'd quit going to church because she wasn't comfortable with God. He'd quit on his friends because hobnobbing and networking with people "in the biz" was more important. Jillie Lynn had taken over his life until she left town and left him with an apartment full of soured memories. He was the silly one to upend his dreams for a life that wasn't what he wanted. Now he had to decide what to do once Sam was settled.

"Cole? Please forgive me." Sam drew closer. Her laughter had silenced. If she were his girlfriend, he would have reached out and hugged her. "I shouldn't have asked, and I wasn't nice." Sam's eyes glistened as if she might cry. Seemed as if she had more regret than Jillie Lynn. "I was curious because Chester's tongue could have licked the drive when he mentioned her." Sam studied the plate of cookies as though deciding on a frosting color.

Why was Sam remembering Chester's reaction? Did it matter what a girlfriend of his looked like? Sam was beautiful. God had put her together rather nicely. Was she jealous in some way? Was that hurt in her eyes? All he wanted was to hear her laughter again and wipe away her nerves.

"You're forgiven. And you're right. Jillie Lynn isn't a common name. And I don't care if I don't hear it again either." He nodded with enthusiasm feeling as if he was back in grade school. He snitched a cookie and made delicious noises as he ate it to show her he was fine. "I'd better get the garbage cans."

"Applicable topic, don't you think?" She gave him a sassy wink and headed toward the front door.

Her spunk was back full throttle. He marched toward the shed. As he reached the shed's door, he turned toward the house. Sam was almost on the porch. Should he ask about a boyfriend? Was it too bold? Nah. Not after she trampled Silly Jillie. He wanted to know if there was a chance at...a possibility at…something, anything. He was curious about her relationship status.

"Hey," he called.

She whirled around.

"Is there a guy with water in his trunk in Wisconsin?"

Her head flew back as she barked a laugh. She held up the package of hot dogs. "See these franks? If we didn't have them for dinner, I'd put a skewer in my last boyfriend and roast him over the fire. While drinking a double latte."

A double latte, deadbeat boyfriend? He could fill a notebook with her lines.

"If it's all right with you, let's stick with roasting the hot dogs."

Sam flashed a thumbs-up sign as she strode into Ted's house.

Lifting the garbage cans, he set one by his truck and headed toward the broken window to leave a can for Sam. He'd use the gator to drag the trunk and limbs away. A sparrow hop, hop, hopped on the broken porch railing tweeting a tune. For the first time in weeks, he felt like singing along.

~*~

Cole brushed the last of the glass shards from his leather driver's seat into a dustpan and then dumped the mess into the garbage can by his truck. With the porch void of tree limbs, he could see Sam's head above a sheet she was trying to hang in the broken window. He should offer to help, but Sam was one determined lady, and he didn't want her to think he thought she was helpless. Not after the embarrassment on her face when she revealed that she lived with her parents. What was the big deal? He knew a few women who still lived at home, and they hadn't been in the hospital. Perfectly fit and healthy was how he would describe his branch-toting partner. She didn't seem sick.

Their earlier conversation about family pestered his conscience. When was the last time he had called his parents? Had it been a month ago? Around the time his mom sent the devotional. He probably hadn't even thanked her for it. He meant to, and then Jillie Lynn had shocked his heart.

I can do everything through Christ who gives me strength. He slumped into the swept-clean driver's seat. Even call his parents? He should let his dad know about Ted. Waiting to share that news would be a bad move. Could he handle questions about Jillie Lynn? Who was he kidding? His parents would pop a cork at the break-up news.

Cole removed his glove, wiped his hand on his jeans, and picked up his phone. His hand smelled like warm cow hide as he speed-dialed his parents' landline in Nashville.

"Cole!" Elation filled his mom's greeting.

"Hey, Mom."

"Mike, Cole's on the phone." His mom's voice

sounded farther off. "Go pick up in the den. Is everything OK?" Her concern was loud and clear. Why shouldn't it be? He rarely called. She might think something was wrong.

"Yeah." He was OK—barely.

"I'm surprised you called with thirty-eight seconds left in the fourth quarter when our team is driving." His dad's statement held a sliver of castigation. Even the timing of Cole's phone call wasn't right. If his life was in normal mode, he'd be coaching football from his sofa and not sweeping shards out of his truck.

"Wish I was at home watching the game. I'm actually in Whispering Creek."

"Ted and your girlfriend finally putting you to work?" His dad emphasized the physical labor before chuckling. A spike of heat coursed through Cole's muscles.

"Oh, Mike. Let Cole talk."

Cole's heart boomed in his chest. Bad news was best given straight and fast, or his dad would have something else to criticize. He gripped the top of the steering wheel. "I'm sorry to have to tell you this, Dad, but Ted passed away."

"What? When?" His dad's voice was almost as expressive as his mom's. "We were talking this morning at Bible Study about messaging him. He hadn't videoed with us lately. Such a shame."

"I only found out when I arrived. I left a message that I was coming, but of course, Ted didn't respond. He had a heart attack a few weeks back." Ernie had given Cole a few details after the drive was cleared.

"We're so sorry, Cole." His mom's words quivered. "How did Jillie Lynn take the news?"

Straightening in his leather seat, he leaned forward and scanned the darkening sky through his maimed windshield. Here came the truth. He braced for the we-told-you-so comments. His mom would hide her pleasure. She would feel Cole's hurt. His dad would add another mark to Cole's poor decisions list.

Bombs away. "Jillie Lynn's not here. We're not together anymore. Our lives were going in different directions." *She beelined it for a country music millionaire and stuck me with her commitments.*

The squeak of his dad's lounger carried through the phone. Cole braced for a lecture.

"Oh." His dad did brief best. "Hey, is Whispering Creek near Sperry's Crossing?"

What?

"Mike, you can talk business later." Chastisement came through the phone loud and clear. "How are you feeling about the breakup, Cole? I know you and Jillie Lynn were together for a long time. And now Ted's gone. I'll be praying extra hard for you." He couldn't have asked for a better mom. If only his dad could be more like Ted. "Why don't you come over after church tomorrow? I'm preparing a roast."

At the mention of Sunday dinner, saliva pooled in his mouth. He needed to make that campfire to cook his hot dog supper.

"I'd love that, Mom." Memories of roasting meat with a hint of garlic and cayenne pepper materialized in his mind. His stomach growled. "But I'm stuck in Whispering Creek for a few days. A storm came through and took down some trees. Powerlines, too. They're blocking Ted's bridge. I spent the day clearing a driveway for Ted's brother. He lives close. On the other side of the lane."

"Do you have any food or water?" his mom asked. "We could bring you some." What was it with mothers and stomachs?

He could hear his mom's worry index rising. Time to calm the concern. "Ted's brother gave us some food. The electric company hopes to have everything cleared by Monday at the latest."

"Us?" His dad never missed a detail.

Cole rubbed his forehead. An ache began to settle there with his father's name on it. Why was he embarrassed to mention Sam to his dad? As if summoned by his conversation, Sam walked onto the porch and surveyed the yard. He waved and gave her a thumbs-up. Her sheet hanging duty had been conquered.

"Cole?" his mom said.

"Sorry. I'm stranded here with the woman who inherited Ted's home. My truck and her house received some damage in the storm. We've been on clean-up duty, and it looks as though she just finished securing the broken window. I'd better hurry and start our campfire so we can eat."

"I'm sure she's glad to have the help," his dad stated the obvious. "Make yourself useful." Cole had been doing that all day. "What's her name so the guys can pray for her?" Inspector Dad was at it again.

"Her name's Sam. Samantha. She was like a granddaughter to Ted and his wife. She drove here from Wisconsin."

"Oh, my. I bet she's glad you showed up for a visit. How scary for you both." If his mom only knew about their dash to the tub. "The Lord watched over you and Sam. Is she your age?"

The matchmaking had begun. "She's a few years younger. She graduated college a year or two ago and started teaching." Change of subject. "And Dad, I passed Sperry's Crossing on the way here. It's about a half hour from Whispering Creek."

"Good to know. Your brother has one of the final bids to do some electrical out that way. New industrial park is going up. Wade is always looking to expand the business."

And this is why he rarely called. The conversation always included Wade even when it didn't have to. Wade was his dad's right-hand man at Donoven and Son. Why shouldn't he be? The company was named after his dad and Wade. They never added an 's' to Donoven and Son when Cole joined the business. Wade won his father's accolades. Cole won advice on how to do his job better…to be like Wade.

"Awesome." Cole swallowed past an ache in his throat. "I'd better go. I need to make a campfire so we can eat. I've got a wiener roast to attend, but it won't be near as good as your cooking, Mom."

"I'm so glad you called. We'll have to get together when you return to Nashville." His mom's voice broke.

"We love you." Now, she was crying.

Darn if his eyes didn't sting. "Love ya'll, too."

"Yep." His dad's response sounded as though he was caught up in the post-game analysis. "Sorry to hear about Ted."

Cole ended the call and tilted his head back against the truck's headrest. The last three weeks had been so crazy that finding out his friend had died, surviving a microburst, and chain-sawing felled trees was a relief from painful memories. Being stranded was a tropical oasis.

Sam paraded along the porch in her hiking boots and dress bending to pick up pieces from the tree, window, roof, and porch. Her hair blocked her pretty face every time she found debris. No complaints erupted into the darkening late-afternoon sky. No demands sailed his way. No insults, or critiques either. He liked simple. He liked Sam.

With his truck cleaned, it was time to start a fire, eat some food, and reassemble the remnants of his life. He grabbed his guitar case and traipsed toward the porch, hoping a firelit evening with Sam could rewrite the tarnished memories of the last few weeks.

Sam sauntered toward him. A flashlight illuminated her figure. What an efficient memory scrubber. Perhaps she'd spill the beans about her ex-boyfriend. Baked beans. Ranch beans. Refried beans.

His stomach gurgled again.

OK, no more food talk until that fire raged, his stomach filled, and he found out more about his intriguing hostess.

9

Sam peeked out the kitchen window at Cole. Light from a robust fire brightened her house guest's rugged features. He sure looked fine in a backward baseball cap and snug t-shirt. Sparks and glowing embers floated into the evening sky illuminating the clearing at the side of Ted's house. With all the rain and the engorged creek, she didn't worry about a brush fire. She had enough to worry about with a damaged inheritance and misshapen body. Sam breathed in the comforting aroma of the woodsy smoke. Immediately, she was transported to summer camp. Late nights talking about boys, bug bites, and God. She wished she had some friends in the room to talk about her new friend Cole. Was her attraction to Cole due to circumstances? He did save her life. Could her feelings for him be heightened by her breakup? Would it even matter how she felt if he found out she was missing a breast from cancer?

Taking a deep breath, she forced the fear to leave her mind. Why was it that every time she thought of cancer, a dread overcame her as if the beast was waiting to claim some other part of her already maimed body. Or worse, take her life away. *God, please don't let any cancer return.* Her oncologist was confident that her system was clear of the mutant cells. Could a doctor ever be sure it wouldn't come back? "A rare occurrence" one specialist had assured her. She wished that simple sentence offered more hope that her cancer was gone for good.

Cole opened the package of hot dogs and speared a few with a stick. Her stomach was beyond hungry. If truth be told, she could tear open the package with her teeth and chomp a hot dog lukewarm. Weren't they filled with enough preservatives to withstand a disaster? She chuckled. Well, they had withstood one storm in Gretta's refrigerator.

Hoping to spare her phone's battery, she picked up a flashlight from the kitchen counter. She filled a bag with paper towels, water bottles, and some newly expired string cheese before heading outside to join Cole. She'd mentioned her hospitalization, and he hadn't pried for a diagnosis. Was he being a gentleman? What if he didn't care? She hoped he cared a little. She was starting to care too much.

Not that she and Cole would ever be romantically involved, but it would be nice to see if there was a chance for something to grow. Perhaps she could ease into her revelation about being lopsided. Mention the cancer and not the breast removal. Closing her eyes, she prayed. *God, help me to be honest. I don't want to be rejected again.* If her cancer diagnosis sent Cole squealing out of Whispering Creek, then she'd be spared opening up about her infection, the loss of an implant, and the pain of having only one breast. Cole didn't seem like her ex, Karlton Coward, but she had to know. *Hang in there, heart.*

She jogged down the porch steps and made her way to Cole's makeshift firepit. A wide branch perched near the circle of rocks became a nice bench for Cole. A guitar case rested a fair distance from the flames. If he serenaded her tonight, she might never ever leave Whispering Creek.

Cole raised his roasting stick in the air. "These dogs are almost done. You're just in time."

His joyous smile made her believe he was offering her a grilled feast. When was the last time a man had been exuberant to see her? She shook the thought from her mind. The aroma of Cole's cooked meat made her want to shove the whole stick in her mouth.

"I found an addition to our meal. Some cheese." She rummaged in the shopping bag and held up the package of mozzarella. "I also have two water bottles to wash down dinner."

He patted a spot on the log at his side. "I never would have guessed a gal from Wisconsin would bring cheese." A grin curved his lips. "The more to eat, the better. Though, I'd rather be grilling ribeyes and corn."

"Me, too." As she sat, her knee bumped his thigh. Even through his jeans, he was muscled and solid. Strong inside and out. Her stomach flipped and not at the sight of the bubbled, slightly blackened hot dogs coming her way.

"Ladies first." Cole held the roasted wieners in front of her. He dipped his head and flailed his hand as if she were royalty.

Playing along with his contagious humor, she

grabbed a napkin and daintily slipped the top dog off the wooden skewer and bit into the meat. Her tastebuds declared the soft, yet crispy hot dog the best meal ever. Her jaw pulled tight as she swallowed. "This is amazing." Cole was amazing.

His eyebrows raised into his sexy orange and white baseball cap. "It doesn't take much to impress you." He bit into his meal, chewed, and tilted his head. "Not bad. Let's see if you can do as well on the next round."

"Ooh, I love a challenge." She welcomed the distraction. Cole was challenging the safety barriers she had placed around her heart.

After making his meal disappear in seconds, Cole threaded more hot dogs on the stick and handed her the skewer. His playful demeanor sobered. "Hey, I'm sorry if I pried earlier about your boyfriend and the water bottles." He motioned to the bottles she had brought from the house.

Wow, God was timely tonight. She shifted on the slightly damp bark. "Yeah, we should have started out with 'what's your favorite ice cream flavor?' It's been a rocky road for me."

"I would have guessed you were a butter pecan gal."

She shook her head and laughed as she rotated the cooking stick. Cole made everything fun. With the light from the flames dancing across his expressive dark eyes, she couldn't fathom why *that girl* had fled. "I meant life has been a rocky road. I actually prefer mocha chip."

"Ice cream with a jolt of caffeine." His radiant smile rivaled the fire's light. "I like it."

She was starting to like him, so she couldn't ignore the diagnosis that upended her life and tanked her last relationship. Honesty was the best policy even if a potential new friend abandoned you. The scent of burning meat brought her out of her musing. "Oops. Guess I better turn these. You had me thinking about dessert." The future, too.

"No worries. I hear charcoal is good for the blood." He gently moved her stick away from the fire. "I think these are done."

Shifting the top link off the skewer, she offered it to Cole. "You can go first this time." Little did he know that she planned to open up about her war chest— literally. Her cheeks grew hot as her fingers grasped another dog. "My former water boy is riding off with a boisterous barista."

"Ouch." Cole covered his mouth as he chewed.

"Really, though." *You can do this.* Her heartbeat resounded to her ears. "I don't think he could handle that I had cancer." Her mouth felt parched as if she hadn't hydrated all day. "I was diagnosed with breast cancer. That's why I was in the hospital and moved back with my parents."

He rotated on the log so he faced her, wide shouldered and with those inquisitive eyes. "You don't have breast cancer now?" Fortunately, more statement than question filled his response. "I mean, you were tossing branches like it was an Olympic event. And, uh, you look great. Healthy." His gaze darted toward the firepit. "Not cancerous." His nose crinkled. "Should you be eating hot dogs?" He grabbed the skewer from her and bit the last blackened dog without taking it off the stick.

"Hey." She lightly punched his bicep. "I'm being serious here." And darn if some self-pity and bruised ego didn't tingle behind her eyes. No, she couldn't cry. She wasn't weak and helpless. Cancer was in her rearview mirror. She blinked back the moisture threatening to spill down her cheeks and swiped at a renegade tear.

Cole set the skewer on the ground and leaned over, wrapping her in a side-armed hug. "I'm so sorry you had to go through that." Thankfully, he hugged her good side. The normal side.

Half of her face burrowed into the warmth of his chest as the touch of his chin on her scalp nestled her snugly in his embrace. With the woodsy scent emanating from his shirt, she could have stayed like this for hours cherishing the understanding from a stranger that her boyfriend failed to provide. Every ounce of her being fought a weep buried for too long. *Why me, Lord? Why now? Who wants to love me now?* And who had ever told her they were sorry for her? Besides her parents, no one. Not even her boyfriend. "Boy, this is tough," Karlton had bemoaned. Now, she wondered if Karlton meant that for her or for him.

She eased away from Cole's warmth not wanting to seem too needy. She was the queen of log throwing after all. But had she shared too much?

Cole's arm remained at her back, firm and

comforting. He picked up the string cheese. "How about some spoiled mozzarella."

Sniffling, she laughed at his ploy to lighten the mood. "They're expired. But totally edible."

"How long have you been boyfriend-free?" Cole's comforting arm slid away as he stripped plastic from their second course of dinner. She missed the kindness in his touch.

Not long. "Since Thursday at lunchtime." Would Cole think she was on the rebound?

"Three days?" He handed her the first roll of cheese. "I think you need this more than me. After three days, I was laying around in bed." His leg jiggled as if he readied to run from this topic. "I didn't get a good-bye. I got a note on my kitchen table. Had to figure out what I had done to get left for another man. I'm not sure I ever will know the answer." His gaze glanced over her head and out into the tree-lined moonlight.

This wasn't Christian of her, but in Sam's book, Jillie Lynn became lower than a nightcrawler. How did you ghost someone as sweet as Cole?

"If I'm honest." She swallowed a hunk of cheese, nearly choking. "Our relationship had been strained for months. Karlton traveled to cement a law firm offer—"

"Your ex was an attorney named Karlton?" Cole stroked his chin while a grin played with his mouth. "I don't know whether to laugh or to punch the guy."

Cole's protective streak had her sitting tall on the wooden bench. "A week ago, I would have said laugh, but today, I'm OK with a punch. Nothing too bloody."

"Man, your boyfriend leaves, and then you find out about Ted?"

"A half-hour later." She jabbed an unwrapped cheese stick his direction. "And while I was on the phone with Chester, I saw Karlton and his neighbor holding hands as they walked across his apartment complex." Rehashing Karlton's betrayal to a handsome friend didn't seem so bad. Cole had more emotional awareness in his thumb than her ex did in his entire designer-suited body. "How's that for a neat, tidy bow?"

Cole's gaze met hers and captivated it. "My bow was seeing Jillie Lynn kissing a music star on television."

The warmth from the fire grew ten times hotter. She playfully jabbed his shoulder. "You win." She stood and threw out her arms. A small piece of mozzarella shot into the flames. "But look at us now. We survived a storm, helped elderly neighbors, roasted the best meal ever."

Shaking his head, Cole slapped his thigh. "You had me until best meal ever." He stood and meandered over to his guitar case. "How about I play a bit? Not only did my ex vanish in the night, she left me contractually obligated to write a song."

"You're a songwriter?" How much cool factor could one guy have? "When you told Chester that you were a writer, I assumed you were an author or worked for a newspaper."

He unlatched the case and took out a guitar. "I

was the studious, dull guy?"

"Your entrance certainly wasn't dull."

"Do you listen to country music?" His strumming sent a comforting melody onto the tepid breeze.

"Not if I can help it. My dad likes it, but all I hear are songs about break ups, glory days, and favorite whiskeys." She stifled a grin. "I'll pass on the lyrics about broken hearts."

"So, you do know country music?" His head bobbed, motioning for her to sit back down. When he straddled the branch, and plucked a few chords, his smile returned. His perfect, genuine, fill-you-up smile. That grinning face needed to end up in a song. And she'd keep that thought to herself.

Cole hadn't fled from her physically or emotionally after her cancer revelation, and he made her believe she could be the woman she was before her diagnosis. Carefree. Confident. Secure in her body. God loved her no matter what she looked like. Too bad some men focused on appearances. One plus, she could hide her imperfection, for now. Hopefully, if she ever did reveal her loss of a breast to Cole, he could see past the deformity.

When the fire burned low, Cole halted his music and returned his guitar to its case. She leaned forward and hugged her waist, missing the soothing melodies and the closeness of someone who accepted her, scars and all.

"Do you mind if I grab a pillow for my truck?" He rubbed his hands together as if he lived in the frozen tundra.

"Truck? You're not sleeping out here." How could she let her rescuer sleep with the mosquitoes and contort his six-two frame in a cramped seat? "Ted has plenty of rooms." Her voice sounded out of tune after Cole's restful chords.

"Yeah, but—"

If they hadn't been warming by a fire, she would swear Cole was blushing. "My front window is a bedsheet. Your truck is missing most of its windshield. It's like we're already sleeping in the same space." She rose, placed a hiking boot on their log bench and planted a fist on her hip for emphasis. "Take the room you had before. Think of it as Christian charity." The doors did lock, and Ted would want her to be hospitable to a friend. His friend, and hers.

"You're sure?"

She couldn't leave Cole scrunched in a truck while she had two empty rooms. "I'm sure."

He placed his guitar case on the log and leaned against the top of the case. "Hey. Thanks for sharing about the cancer and your ex. I can't think of why anyone would want to hurt you. And I can't understand why anyone would let you go."

Tears puddled in her eyes. Someone who had been a stranger hours before, showed more kindness and understanding than a boyfriend she'd dated for close to two years. "Thank you. And I'll bounce those words right back to you." She picked up her flashlight along with the bag and the uneaten cheese. She aimed a round circle of light at his chest. "You know, you could use those lines as country lyrics. You should have brought a notebook to our starlit confessions."

"If only I had a warning that our campfire would turn into a confessional, I'd have been all over it." With a soft smile, he gave a quick nod. "Good night, Sam."

She turned and headed toward the porch. "Sleep tight, Cole."

Entering Ted's room, her new room, she sat on the bed. Her feet ached as if she had run a marathon, but she was so energized, she could twirl around the bedroom. Cancer hadn't scared Cole. He was caring and open and honest. Would he be as accepting of her when she shared about her loss?

Ted's Bible rested on the nightstand. She should read Scripture and praise God for watching over her. Again. The prayer warriors at church had bombarded Him with requests since her diagnosis. Opening the Bible to the book of Psalms, a picture fell from the pages and fluttered to the floor. Reaching for the photo, she recognized Ted holding a guitar and a handsome songwriter smiling with her friend and pointing at the neck of the guitar. Cole's honest spirit shone through the photograph and stroked her heart. Darn if that sting wasn't back in her eyes. She missed Ted and Nan and the days in her childhood when life was carefree. No decisions had to be made about careers, surgeries, where to live, and who to share life with.

If Ted was praying for Cole, then she would, too. She wished Ted could tell her his concerns, and why Cole needed prayer. But then, she held her secrets close to her chest, too. A deformed chest in need of healing.

10

Cole listened to the clomp of Sam's boots until they faded into Ted's home. He'd been in Whispering Creek one day and not only did he survive a microburst of wind, he'd survived a tornado of emotions. Fright from the storm. Guilt at being coerced to help Ernie. Satisfaction with his labor. Sadness over time wasted with Jillie Lynn. Anger at a selfish ex-boyfriend attorney. Most surprising was the connection he shared with a shapely acquaintance turned partner and friend.

He kicked dirt into the dying embers while keeping his guitar case away from the dust. Enough stars illuminated the sky, casting shadows on Ted's porch and the shed where two windswept trees rested for the night. The root balls of the evergreens had been unearthed, leaving the trees to die a slow death, unless someone in town needed a Christmas tree. Sam could use one to make her living room festive. That is, if she was staying in Whispering Creek and not racing back to Wisconsin.

Balancing his weight on the top of his black leather guitar case, the felled bench giving it height, he remained motionless. His feet didn't trudge toward the house. His fingers didn't strum another song. He was stuck. Life had come to forks in the road, and he didn't know which path to take. Or who he wanted to be. Unlike the battered trees, he couldn't trust his future to a homeowner with a chainsaw.

The serenade of a bullfrog disturbed the tranquil night as if he had advice for Cole on the future. "Sorry, Dude. I don't listen to fly eaters."

A raindrop plopped on his nose. Perfect. A cool dousing before bed. Cole scanned the sky for a threatening cloud, but none existed. A chill rippled across his skin. Was the man upstairs trying to get his attention?

He swiped the moisture from his nose. "You know, I'm not happy with you, God. Right after I casually mention that maybe JL and I should find a church, she leaves me. I come out here to Ted's place to hear more of his wisdom, and You took him too." His knuckles throbbed where he gripped the guitar case. "And I meet the sweetest girl, and You gave her cancer. Why? None of this makes sense."

Silence.

What was he expecting? An answer? "Why don't You release a downpour, God?"

Breathing in the air so pure and peaceful, he fumed. What were his options at present? Go back to his dad and brother and grovel for an income. They banished him to service calls and strategized the business without him. No wonder writing pathetic heartbreak songs wooed him away. He stared at a winking star. "I handled my last relationship badly. And now, you send me another girl, and she might as well live in a different country. Wisconsin. Isn't that almost Canada?"

I'm losing it.

I can do everything through Christ who gives me strength.

His chuckling shut up the boisterous bullfrog. "I have plenty of strength, Lord, but I don't know what things You want me to do. I don't know what I want to do. Help me write one last song, and then my future is all Yours. Surprise me. Just don't kill anyone or give them cancer."

A fat droplet doused his chin.

"OK, I was a little disrespectful on that last part. I'm speaking from the heart and being real. I've kind of forgotten how to do that prayer acronym. Deal?" He surveyed the sparkling stars he could see between clouds. God didn't answer but the bullfrog screeched something fierce. Maybe it was mating season.

He hefted his guitar and headed for the house. Being a bullfrog was a less stressful life. Halting, he raised a hand toward the indigo heavens. "Only joking there, Lord."

Wasn't he a handy guy? A doer. Chop up a tree with a single chainsaw kind of guy. He could do things. If only he could figure out what things made him happy.

11

Sam got out of the bed and flipped the nearest light switch. Nothing. Still no electricity. Her phone glared 9:01 AM. Arching her back, she prayed, "It's Sunday, Lord. Can we please get some running water?" She had caught herself a few times before trying to flush the toilet.

Not a floor squeak or a glass clink came from the kitchen or living room. Cole must be sleeping. She didn't blame him after all the debris removal he had done the day before.

She rummaged through her suitcase and pulled on jeans and a pink long-sleeve shirt. After brushing her hair, she tied it in a ponytail, and tiptoed through the living room with Ted's Bible in hand. Had the bridge been miraculously cleared of trees during the night? She opened the front door and pushed past the screen. A delightful morning breeze greeted her, but the grind of construction equipment was absent.

Hand on her hip, she descended the porch steps and stared down the drive. Dying leaf clusters and wayward sticks marred the sleek black lane. An eerie peacefulness settled over the pine trees as if she and Cole were the only people on earth. Life continued on for others, but she was stuck, trapped with her inheritance. Her inner motor churned, wanting to get her to-do list done. It was Sunday, a day for church, but her worship plans were useless. She would read her Bible and pray at the kitchen table today. *Lord, we really need some power and the bridge cleared.*

Returning inside, she headed to the dinette table and set down her Bible. Cole had emptied his truck of a lighter, so she lit some candles. Her breakfast options consisted of Cole's opened package of red-hot candy, his chocolate bar, or her box of granola bars. An ache in her forehead pulsed a low-caffeine warning. Unless Cole built another fire and they heated coffee like cowboys in the Old West, lukewarm cans of Ted's sodas would have to suffice.

Easing the tab open on her soda, she sipped the syrupy fizz and envied anyone ordering a Grande Colombian brew. Cole's dark chocolate bar called her name. A small piece might help calm her burgeoning headache. She unwrapped the bar and broke off a square. The soothing rich taste of cocoa jumpstarted her day, until her tongue began to burn. Was the chocolate tainted? She swished more warm drink in her mouth and broke open a granola bar. Crunchy oats banished the burning sensation. Then, she spotted it. What should have been in bright red lettering on the chocolate wrapper was buried beneath the lure of organic chocolate—flavored with chili. Who ruins chocolate with spice? And who enjoys a scalding mouth? Cole. The man didn't do bland food. If she focused on her house guest too much, she would be distracted during her devotions.

Sitting at the table, she opened Ted's Bible. A large number four in the book of Philippians stared at her. Verse four caught her attention.

Rejoice in the Lord always. I will say it again: Rejoice!

A bubble of laughter filled the stillness. "Lord, I'd rejoice this morning to step into a shower." Joy had been less than abundant as she ping-ponged from a breakup to news of Ted's death, to an exhausting trip, to surviving a storm, and to securing a house she inherited in a different state. She didn't even know how large the deductible was on the homeowner's insurance or if Chester had switched the policy. A pang of guilt sobered her complaints. She should rejoice that her time without power and water was limited, and not unending like so many places in the world.

The next verses in Philippians were as challenging as their predecessor.

Let your gentleness be evident to all. The Lord is near. Do not be anxious about anything, but in everything, by prayer and petition, with thanksgiving, present your requests to God.

She tilted her face toward the eggshell-white ceiling. "How can I not be anxious, Lord? I have a house to repair in Tennessee. I need to schedule reconstructive surgery in Wisconsin." And what about Cole? She had met him less than twenty-four hours ago, and he had become a rainbow in her overcast world. She liked Cole, but what was the use of thinking about a relationship? When the bridge cleared and his windshield and wheel were fixed, he'd be high-tailing it back to Nashville. Poof. Gone.

A thought hit her. Was Cole a guardian angel? She rubbed her pounding temples. She cast a glance at the opened chocolate bar. No angel left chili infused chocolate for a stressed female to find.

Verse seven of Philippians.

And the peace of God, which transcends all understanding, will guard your hearts and your minds in Christ Jesus.

Peace. She slumped against the wooden slats of the chair. "I know I have eternal peace, Lord. Right now, it's my temporary peace that has fled. It's like I'm crossing a dilapidated suspension bridge between two cliffs, and I'm coming to a section that has boards missing. Help me find peace right now. Before Christmas." She closed her eyes. Covering her face with her hands, she leaned on the tabletop and basked in the intimacy with her Lord.

Footsteps echoed in the hallway.

Cole strode toward her wearing jeans and a tight gray tee. His dark hair was best described as tamed bed head. The shadow of a beard accentuated his ruggedness as an endearing smile spread across his face.

She straightened and forced a "Good Morning" in her authoritative teacher voice to camouflage the tutu twirl in her belly. With every nerve in her body sensing Cole's approach, the morning was anything but peaceful. Had he heard her prayers? She was sure that he was too far away to hear her confessions. Warmth spread from her neckline into her cheeks. "I, uh, saved you some caffeine." She held up his can of soda.

"Thanks." He opened the drink and grabbed a granola bar. "I'm not usually up this early."

"I know what you mean. I'm usually at church."

"I should be too." He nodded toward her Bible. "But you brought church with you."

"Thanks to Ted leaving one on his nightstand." She glanced to make sure the picture of Cole was secured in the pages of the Old Testament. No one deserved an inquisition before swigs of caffeine.

Her houseguest perched himself in the chair next to her. Not the one at the end of the table. Not the one a few yards away. He was close enough that she could pop him a friendly punch. And he was close enough that a faint hint of campfire smoke radiated from his body reminding her of his gentle hug. His wide-legged posture and slight lean in her direction had her desiring to dive into his arms again. Where was a storm alert when you needed one?

God, I need peace here. "I'm reading Philippians. It's the P in 'Go Eat Pop Corn.' Galatians, Ephesians. Philippians. Colossians. That's how we memorized the books of the Bible in Sunday school." She was babbling.

Cole jerked slightly, an alertness widening his eyes. "I can do everything through Christ who gives me strength. Philippians four thirteen."

"Well, I'm impressed." Could this guy get any more perfect?

"Don't be. My Mom sent me a devotional with that verse on the cover. I never cracked open her gift.

The spark in his gaze dimmed. "Truth is, I've been avoiding talking to God." The aluminum can crinkled under Cole's grip.

Not that woman again. "Because of your breakup?"

"Some." He faced her, full frame, bringing the alluring vulnerability of Cole. A bond of connection bore down on her, and in this moment, she was free falling off that imaginary suspension bridge, and she didn't care what lay below.

"It goes back longer than her." He shifted the Bible towards himself. His gaze darted to the big four on the page and he read some of the verses. Silence hung in the air. A silence of reminiscing and recollection. "Guess I need to pray and petition because these past few weeks haven't been filled with much peace."

"For you and me both." She toasted him with her caffeinated drink and took a sip. Cole didn't join in her false revelry. He stared at the Scripture as though he was reading the text in Greek. His expression matched the drab gray of the storm.

"Maybe we could pray?" The question was off her lips before she could analyze whether Cole would happily agree or be pushing his chair to the opposite end of the room.

"Yeah. Let's go for it." The response was typical Cole. Overcast to sunshine in a second. He reached over and offered her his palm.

Twice, within hours, he had lifted her spirits, offering acceptance and teamwork. She took hold of his hand as if it was a lifeline. The warmth of his touch and firmness of his grasp, made her want to tuck the sensation away for later and always. Why couldn't she have had this caring, this affirmation, when she was in the hospital? Her mom hovered over her tending to every medical need, flitting to the nurse's station when pain meds were overdue. Her dad offered a pat on the shoulder. She didn't blame him for the awkwardness, for what father delights in discussing breast removal with a daughter? Karlton visited after surgery and may as well have been wall scaffolding for as close as he got to her bed. Cole's openness, his welcoming nature, made her feel alive and whole even though she wasn't fully healed, emotionally. She forced a smile through the memories. "Do you want me to pray? I mean, you could join in. We could pray together."

"You begin. I may only add an Amen, but I'll have my listening ears on." He bowed his head. His hair hung over his eyes, but she noticed a grin emblazoned across the lower half of his face.

"Dear God." Her brain jumbled with requests. "Thank you for watching over Cole and me. Ernie and Gretta, too. We pray that the bridge may be cleared today and that our power may be restored. Cole's truck and my window need a lot of help." How personal should she get in her prayer? Her body temperature rose fifty degrees. Was her palm sweating? *Focus on God*. "Life has been crazy for Cole and me recently. Please give us wisdom and strength to make decisions about our, uh, the future."

"And God." Cole jumped right in. She added a silent prayer that he missed any allusion to a relationship.

"Thank you for healing Sam."

A gentle squeeze snuggled her hand. Such a small gesture, but it was enough to take a sledgehammer to her fragile state. She clenched her teeth and willed her eyes to stay dry.

"Bless this day," Cole continued. "Amen."

"Amen." She raised her head, slipped her hand from Cole's, and positioned her ponytail like this was an average, ordinary prayer and not one that she would cherish for a long time.

Cole grabbed another granola bar and quickly re-read the passage in Philippians. When he was done speed reading, he glanced her way. "Man, could I go for some bacon and eggs with a side of hot sauce."

Lights in the kitchen flickered.

She held her breath.

"God, is that you?" Cole's head tilted heavenward. "Can I add a firm banana and decent coffee?"

The house brightened. Every light they had forgotten to turn off beamed with electricity.

"Praise the Lord." Now, she could shower and flush the toilet and brew some caffeine.

Pushing his chair away from the table, Cole stilled. His forehead wrinkled. "Is that what I think it is?" He leapt to his feet and jogged out the front door, halting on the porch. As she approached, she heard it, too. A faint, rhythmic beeping. Warning sounds of heavy equipment backing up. Someone was working out by the road.

God had sure made short work of their prayer.

With access to the property, Cole could get his truck towed, a claims adjustor could evaluate the damage to the porch, roof, and window, and she could even rendezvous with her attorney.

Cole shaded his eyes from the Sunday morning sun. "Life is back on." He hurried down the porch steps and strode toward the bridge. Suddenly, he stopped and started to backstep, facing her. "We need to pray more often." Exuberance heightened his boy-next-ranch handsomeness and caused her stomach to ache.

"Well, we did ask for a blessing and breakfast." She gave him a thumbs-up. Life was moving forward. Fast forward for Cole. Slow motion for her. He'd be able to leave Whispering Creek, but she had responsibilities holding her here.

Do not be anxious. Do not be anxious. Do not be anxious. About anything.

She mentally kicked herself as she followed Cole down the asphalt driveway, her hiking boots scuffing over bits of leftover storm reminders. Her short prayer when she rolled out of bed should have been about more than needing a shower. It should have been about what to do with this man who had barged into her life and chicken-fried her heart. Or how she could help him heal the wounds he couldn't voice. The wounds that leapt from the picture Ted had hidden in his Bible. Whatever came her way, she would cherish her morning prayer time with Cole and carry her prayers for him into tomorrow.

Rejoice in the Lord.

I know, Lord, but I'm warning You. My heart's going to need some simple surgery when I witness his taillights heading down my busted bridge.

12

The tow truck driver hummed a tune as he attached a hook to the front axle of Cole's truck. "It's a good thing you didn't call yesterday afternoon. I was slammed." A gray washed design of a cross tattoo became visible on the driver's upper arm. He turned to watch Sam as she paced on the porch, phone to ear. The roar of the lift was almost as obnoxious as the young dude's stare. Cole rubbed a fist in his palm instead of planting it into the guy's face.

"Yeah, well we were stuck when the bridge was blocked." Cole emphasized *we* hoping driver dude took the hint of a relationship. A relationship that wasn't defined, but the tow operator didn't need to know the facts. Sam would be staying at the house alone tonight with a sheet for a window. Cole's gut twisted. A muscular dude was eyeing Sam as if she were the powdered sugar on a brownie, but what could he do? With the bridge cleared, and his vehicle in town, he didn't have a reason to stay at Ted's place.

"I need a signature." The driver thumbed the screen on his computer and extended it to Cole. The dude rolled his shoulders as if he thought he was in a bodybuilding competition. "Is that your girlfriend?" He tipped his head in Sam's direction and used the same monotone "sign here" voice.

Cole didn't want to lie, but telling the truth made him downright sick. Would Sam even be interested in this guy? Was the cross tattoo an indication that he was a strong Christian? *Help me here, Lord.* Cole signed in the slowest manner possible. Think.

"If I called her old, I'd be sleeping in the shed." Cole grinned as he emphasized the sleeping part of the sentence. He was fairly confident the driver would take the hint, and he was somewhat confident he wasn't telling a lie about the shed.

"Does the body shop know it's comin'?" the driver asked, his attention settling on Cole's face and not on Sam's curves.

Yes! "Yes," Cole cleared his throat. "They know about the damage to the wheel and the missing glass."

On protocol, Cole tipped the dude and stood in the middle of the drive, arms crossed, acting as though he were the man of the house while the tow truck drove away, bathing him in acrid diesel fumes.

"Are you ready for lunch? It's too late for church." Sam dangled her keys as if trying to hypnotize him. He was desperate for caffeine and would have raced her to town or even accepted a ride from the tattooed tow guy. "I don't know what's worse. Hunger or listening to Emma explain about storm coverages. That girl is best friends with too many search engines."

"I'm ready for brunch, lunch, and supper." He jogged toward her SUV. Grabbing the handle, he stilled. Since they were going into Whispering Creek proper, he should bring his duffle bag and guitar. Sam could drop him off at a motel or at a rental car agency. The excitement of being freed from captivity waned. Soon he would say good-bye to his newest friend. One who made him feel as if he had conquered the world by sawing a tree. He tapped his boot, finding his foot heavy. Turning, he said, "I should probably pack my things. We'll be in town." Score one for being a gentleman.

Sam's shoulders sagged as she trudged toward him. She huffed with exasperation. "My head is pounding. It's so bad that I almost ate more of your flaming chocolate and sticky candy. We can talk about your stuff later."

"Suit yourself." He jumped into the passenger seat of her SUV savoring his small victory of spending a few more hours with Sam. He knew better than to come between a cranky female and sugar, chocolate, or caffeine.

~*~

Cole let out a long whistle as they cleared the bridge and turned right. Electrical trucks dotted the side of the country road. Trees that had once bordered the creek were flattened into the mud. Red and blue lights from a police car flashed ahead where arborists worked clearing branches.

"Whoa." Cole scratched his stubbled jaw. "You know those verses about God guarding our hearts and our minds. I think he guarded Ted's house too."

"And Ernie's." Sam hunched closer to the steering

wheel peering at a man in a tree trimming bucket. "This is insane. I don't want to think about what might have happened to us."

"The bridge is still standing. That's something to rejoice in. The railing, not so much."

Sam glanced his direction. Her hazel eyes had a green hue and looked more refreshed. "Thank you, Cole."

"For what?" She was the one who'd housed him overnight and was driving him into town.

"For being my own personal tree trimmer. I don't know what I would have done if you hadn't arrived in Whispering Creek."

"You would have survived." He should thank God for that blessing. "You're a survivor. You beat cancer." Sam gave him a half-hearted smile and concentrated on the road. "Besides, God would have watched over you." He'd mentioned God's name more in the last few hours than he had in the last year. Or at least since he'd visited Ted last summer.

Sam grinned. "I've been thanking God more in the last two days than I have in the last two months. Tennessee has done wonders for my prayer life."

Whispering Creek and a pretty Yankee had jump started his prayer life.

He pointed to a fork in the road. "Take a right ahead. We'll end up on Main Street. There's a coffee shop not far from here. Ted loved their orange pecan cinnamon rolls."

"Right now, I could eat the whole pan." She flashed him a desperate expression.

Smiling, he said, "Good thing the toilets are working back at the house."

"Cole!"

They laughed.

A few of the cookie-cutter ranch homes outside of town had downed limbs, but nothing like the felled trees by the bridge. The stoplight near downtown flashed red. It probably had a short.

Sam stopped and then drove slowly. "This town is so cute. I love those Christmas wreaths on the streetlights. With all the commotion, I almost forgot Christmas was coming."

"The town has electricity. That's good news for food and coffee." He gestured to an empty parking space on the righthand side of the street. The hardware store's ripped awning flagged the opening in front of the coffee shop. "Grab that parking spot."

Her nose crinkled. "A Brew 4 You. If we were in Wisconsin, I'd be thinking about beer."

"This early? On a Sunday? Shame on you."

Her mouth gaped, and then she grinned.

Teasing her was a blast. She didn't take jokes too seriously or analyze any deeper meaning to start a fight.

She parked the car and cocked her head his direction. "Our baseball team is the Brewers. Coffee isn't the beverage of choice at the ballpark."

"I'm impressed. Sports references before breakfast." He unhooked his seatbelt, enjoying the ease of the banter with Sam. One of the things he had been good at when he worked for his dad was getting to know customers. After a few questions, customers opened up to him about their electrical problems and added their life struggles. He had listened and made notes on his phone in case he returned to their homes. Sam struck him as someone who cared about people. Not only in an emergency, but in day-to-day life. He'd been living in a drought of caring, meeting the demands of his ex, which he now realized wasn't truly living.

Glancing at one of the twinkling wreaths on the lamppost, he shot an arrow prayer to God. *Thank You for making me feel like rejoicing again.*

He followed Sam down the sidewalk, breathing in the fresh air and taking in the fake snow scenes on the store windows. Would Sam be going back to snow? He shivered as though he'd forgotten a coat in a storm. He'd think about good-byes later and why the thought of leaving this place depressed his hopeful mood.

Cole opened the door for Sam and set off a jingle of bells. The coffee shop owner hadn't gotten the memo on Christmas décor. Winter scenes and flickering lights were absent from the storefront.

As they entered the shop, the scent of coffee beans and cinnamon greeted them. He could almost eat the air. His jaw pulled tight thinking about their upcoming meal.

"It smells so good in here." Sam rubbed her hands together. The gesture had to be simple excitement over a meal because she had weathered colder temperatures than fifty-eight degrees.

Simple. Simplify. Hadn't Ted told him last spring

that Cole's life was too crowded with goals that didn't matter in God's Kingdom?

"I'll be with you in a minute. Grab a table." A woman in an apron rushed by. Her dark-brown hair was tied in a bun. The hair at the top looked like an exploding volcano. Had she lost power?

Sam headed to the closest table. Since it was past noon, only half the tables were filled with customers. Obnoxious growling sounds interrupted the din of polite conversation. A young boy played in front of the pastry counter with a plastic dinosaur. The green figurine sailed through the air, and with every roar the kid uttered, Cole's head boomed. Hadn't the boy learned manners in preschool? That toy better not end up in Cole's cinnamon roll, or he'd eat the figurine along with the frosting.

Sam rested her hands on the square wooden table. Her gaze followed the rebel kid. She smiled at his boisterous expressions. Wasn't she wondering where his parents were?

Oh, no. As if by a mysterious teacher spell, the boy held his dinosaur high as if it was show and tell time. He trudged toward their table with an annoying Big Foot impersonation. If Cole didn't get coffee soon, he might roar, too.

The boy hovered near Sam, of course. He held up his dinosaur. "I've got a T-Rex." The men doing tree work outside the bridge could hear this kid.

Sam hunched so she was eye to eye with the terror. "I think I might have a dinosaur sticker in my purse. Would you like one if it's OK with your mom or dad?"

The boy nodded. He followed Sam's every move with wide eyes and closed lips.

Silence was golden. If Sam pulled a sticker out of her purse, then she was definitely an angel.

And she did. Holding a round sticker so the boy could see, she said, "What's your name?"

"Daniel." The enraptured boy did a mini-Hulk move and hopped twice.

"Do you know what type of dinosaur this is?" Sam held the sticker closer.

Shaking his head, the boy shimmied toward Sam's highbacked chair.

"It's like a tiny T-Rex. It's called a velociraptor." Sam accentuated the syllables. "They eat meat just like a T-Rex. And just like my friend, Cole, who roasts hot dogs and shoves them in his mouth." She stifled a laugh, but Cole could tell her giggle dam was about to burst.

Cole rubbed a hand over his jaw, hiding a grin. He received a side-eyed glance from the kid. If the boy was older, he might have seen Cole as competition for Sam's attention.

Sticker lady's mine, kiddo.

Where did that come from? If he was truthful with himself, it sounded rather nice, but he was leaving soon, and he wasn't sure Sam was staying. He really needed caffeine and bacon and pastry.

Sam brought out a small plastic container from her purse. "Would you like to look through my stickers for another dinosaur?" She offered it to the boy. "You could even draw what it eats." Sam pushed her napkin and a fat pen with different colored ink in the kid's direction.

The interrupter nodded. "Pease." He immediately used all his might to push a chair closer to the table and was perched at Sam's side before Cole could get up and help him.

"Daniel, what are you doing?" The volcano-bun lady raced over to their table. Her eyes widened as if she had jolted awake from a bad dream. "I am so sorry."

Praise the Lord. The waitress, whose cockeyed nametag read Lucinda, held a coffeepot and two mugs.

"My mother is ill, and she usually watches Daniel for me. Some of my staff are dealing with storm issues." Lucinda attempted to shift her son's chair away from Sam.

"He's fine, really." Sam reached out and stilled the mother's chair gymnastics. "I'm used to a classroom of eager learners. And we know all about storm damage." Sam shot him a knowing glance. "We were recently sprung from being trapped at Ted Beckman's place."

"Oh, no. Were you friends of Ted's? I was so sorry to hear of his passing. He always gave me a cheerful smile and words of wisdom." Lucinda frowned. She blinked as she poured coffee in each cup, careful to avoid dripping on her son's ruffled hair. The coffee bean aroma almost had him rampaging like a T-Rex.

"Thank you." Sam grew serious. Light from the fixture hanging above their table, glistened in her eyes. "Ted was like my adopted grandfather. He shared a lot of wisdom with me over the years as well. I was planning to visit, and,…well…" Sam swallowed and let out a breath. "Instead, he left me his house."

Lucinda laid a hand on Sam's shoulder. "My condolences. I miss Ted, too."

Cole wished he could come alongside Sam and wrap her in a hug, but Lucinda and Daniel had stationed themselves in the most inconvenient places. He shifted to the edge of his chair and leaned nearer to Sam.

Daniel scribbled on his napkin, oblivious to the adult talk around him.

"If you were stuck at Ted's, then you're probably hungry. Because I'm short on staff, we're doing a scrambled egg and bacon breakfast with our famous cinnamon rolls. Does that work for you two?" Lucinda's gaze rested on him. Had she noticed his frustration with her son?

"Works for me." He lifted his mug. "This coffee sure helps my mood. Warm soda can't compete. I'm practically rejoicing." He winked at Sam who was shaking her head at his enthusiasm for caffeine. Good. He had diverted her attention from Ted's death.

After Lucinda headed to the kitchen, Daniel stopped drawing. He held his scribbles so Sam could see.

"Ooh. Your dinosaur will be able to hide behind that tree." Her expressive eyes almost had him believing the scratches on the napkin were a rendition of the Amazon jungle.

Cole stretched to see the drawing. He didn't want

Sam to think he wasn't interested. He'd been an internal grump since entering the coffee shop.

"Is there a monkey in that tree?" he asked between gulps of caffeine. Before he knew it, a surge of energy shot through his limbs, and he was mimicking chimp sounds and scratching like a monkey.

Sam rolled her eyes.

"You funny." Daniel rocked back and forth in his chair, laughing.

Was he? He used to get compliments from customers about his personality when he fixed their electrical problems and shot the breeze, but lately, his humor had taken a vacation.

Lucinda returned with their plates of food.

"I can get him out of your hair if you'd like." Lucinda bit her lip as if waffling on what to do with her son. "Daniel's dad isn't in the picture, and with my mom...."

"He's not bothering us." Sam's voice was filled with concern. Clearly, her teacher senses were going on high alert. "I'm used to a classroom full of energized students. One on one is not a problem."

Cole picked up a thick slice of bacon. "Daniel can't leave now that you brought us T-Rex food." He bit into the salty cured meat and practically groaned with appreciation. "Thank you for the food, Lord." A simple grace was better than a long one.

Daniel leapt from his chair and hopped into Cole's lap, wiggling for balance. His fingers grabbed a piece of Cole's bacon. "T-Rex meat."

"Daniel! Get off of him," Lucinda chastised.

Cole didn't tell the boy to hop off. He kind of liked that he was considered cool now. "He's OK." That came out fast. Sam was rubbing off on him. "We might need some more T-Rex meat though."

"If you're sure?" Lucinda hesitated, biting her lip.

He cast a glance at Sam. A huge smile covered her face. Not a care from the storm or her inheritance wrinkled her pretty face. If being kind to a little boy brought her joy, then he would entertain Daniel during their breakfast.

"We're sure," he said, and Sam echoed. Cole would have to brush the dust off of his kid skills because unlike Sam, Jillie Lynn wasn't a fan of "germinators."

"I'll get some more dinosaur food right away." Lucinda stifled a smile as she hurried off.

Daniel shifted on Cole's lap. "Do you mind if I put my arm here, buddy?" Cole kept the boy from falling with an arm at Daniel's waist.

The boy shook his mop of hair as if he was ripping a carcass apart.

Sam dipped her head at Daniel, raised her eyebrows, and beheld Cole with a curious grin. "You handled that well."

Cole cocked his head. "Sharing my bacon?"

"Asking permission to place your arm at his waist. You're a natural." She forked some scrambled eggs into her mouth. "You'd make a fantastic teacher."

He broadened his shoulders. He'd only been around Sam for two days, and she had boosted his ego to Mars. Not only did the woman think he was a lumberjack, fire builder, and rescuer, she thought he was a kid tamer, too.

"Thank you." He acknowledged her compliment. *Let us rejoice and be glad in this day.* Hadn't he learned a song like this when he was in Sunday school? He rejoiced when he was around Sam. Was it because of her solid relationship with God? She'd beaten cancer and lost a good friend. Instead of wallowing in pity, she focused on others and made sure they were OK. "I'll leave you to do the teaching." Leaving is what made him anxious. Soon, he would leave Whispering Creek and head back to what? An empty apartment? Writing a song he'd never want to hear?

God, I'm at a crossroads here, and there isn't a lane I feel like taking.

Crunching into orange-flavored pecans, he amused himself. His prayer would make a good line in a heartbreak song.

Heartbreak. He was staying in town tonight. He glanced at Sam. "Maybe I should call the motel. See about a room."

Lucinda set a carafe of coffee on the table. Bless her. "Do you have a room already?"

"Not yet." He acknowledged Lucinda just as Daniel scraped icing and a hunk of cinnamon roll from Cole's plate. The kid knew about distractions.

"They've had some electrical problems. Last I heard they were sending some guests to Hudson." Lucinda swept bangs from her eyes. "I doubt they have any rooms."

Rejoice.

"See, Cole." Sam sipped her coffee. "It's a good thing you didn't pack your stuff. You're coming back to Ted's B&B."

Daniel turned. His big brown eyes perused Cole's face. "Don't leave, Co."

That simple statement seized Cole's heart and almost made him want to cry. For the first time in a long while, it seemed people actually wanted him around.

13

Sam exited the coffee shop while Cole held the door open. The afternoon air outside didn't hold the succulent and comforting aromas of cured meat and cinnamon.

Daniel pressed his drawing to the front window as she passed. She guessed by his wide-open mouth and crinkled nose that he was gracing the restaurant patrons with another rendition of his favorite dinosaur.

She gave the four-year-old a thumbs up and waved.

"Don't encourage him." Cole leaned close to her ear. "He might stow away in your car."

Cole's breath tickled her lobe. She didn't flinch or shift away. She was getting accustomed to having him around. Her house guest handled storms, chainsaws, and chaos with the ease of a Sunday drive. Before Cole arrived, anxiety had been her constant companion. Should she plan another reconstruction surgery? What if it went wrong again? Would she lose another teaching contract and go into more debt? Would it be insensitive to sell Ted's gift to her?

Do not be anxious about anything.

Cole embodied that verse from Philippians. He didn't freak out over the storm. He reacted, rushing them to safety. Not a single curse word was uttered over the damage to his truck. He saw a problem and worked to fix it. Too bad he wasn't around when her health had tumbled into the toilet. Cole's steady, calm wisdom and his strong, capable arms would have done her wonders. She would cherish these last remaining hours before he headed back to Nashville, and she would thank God for sending her a friendly rescuer.

Slowing her steps, she pressed the door button on her key fob while Cole headed to the passenger side of the car. She flashed him a challenging smile. "I wasn't the one who stuffed Daniel full of bacon."

"You mean T-Rex meat." He flashed a five o'clock-shadow grin from across the hood that almost had her roaring.

Raising her eyebrows, she shot him her most accusatory stare. "You were pretty authentic with your growls by the end of brunch." Stifling a laugh, she opened her driver's door. "You know, Cole, I was thinking about their Christmas decorations."

"Or lack thereof."

So, he had noticed. "We have those two trees uprooted by the shed."

His expression mirrored Daniel's when she'd removed the dinosaur sticker from her purse. "I was thinking about those the other night. We could offer one to Lucinda, and you'd still have one for the house."

The house she didn't know what to do with. She had planned to come to Tennessee for a few days. Enough time to meet with Chester, get a check, and leave town. She never dreamed that she would be a homeowner in a different state. Now she had damaged property and enough inheritance business to keep her in Whispering Creek for at least a week and maybe even longer. She still had to go through Ted's belongings.

"Yeah, about that," she said as they buckled their seatbelts. "I'm all in for giving one to Lucinda, but it would be a waste for me to use one." She started the car. "I've always been with my parents on Christmas, praying for a light dusting of snow. I'm hoping the repairs to the window and porch don't take too long and mess up my plans. If I'm not here, it would be a waste of a nice pine tree." And a fire hazard. She didn't need another catastrophe.

"Are you sure you don't want to enjoy it?" Cole's muscular frame filled her passenger seat. "Christmas is only three weeks away."

She checked her mirrors and noticed the streetlamp standing guard by her parking spot. The glass panes were intact, held in place by blackened iron, but a few cracks marred their perfect, quaint appearance. Wasn't that a picture of her life at the moment? She looked perfect from the outside but on the inside, she hid a botched reconstruction surgery that appeared in the mirror every morning. She pasted a carefree smile on her face and masked her complicated thoughts. "I'm thinking maybe Ernie and Gretta could use a tree. We can ask them when we replace the hot dogs they gave us yesterday with a few extra groceries."

"That's right neighborly of you, Wisconsin, but I'm buying seeing as I don't have to pay for a hotel tonight." He was in full-on jokester mode. A full stomach and caffeine had him so amped, she would bet his energy could fuel them back to Ted's place.

"Then let's get a move on." Her Southern drawl earned a D plus. "I know you want to fire up that chain saw."

"You don't mind me playing with your toys?" He was pulling her leg, and she liked it. "Do you have a sticker of a UTV?" Head flung back, he cast a glance at her with those brown eyes that sparked with vigor and a bit of danger. Danger for her beleaguered heart.

"I just might, Officer." She swallowed her grin and checked the rearview mirror before putting her SUV in reverse. She hoped he didn't notice how much she craved his company. Their inevitable good-bye weighed on her mind. The verse about God guarding her heart played over and over in her head.

As she hit the gas pedal on the way to the grocery store, she thought about being back on the imaginary suspension bridge with no sure footing or destination on the other side. But she was determined to grip the rough rope hand holds on the bridge and enjoy her bonus hours with her handsome houseguest.

~*~

Sam flipped on the left turn signal as she approached Ted's bridge. A single tree remained to be trimmed on the side of the road. Most of the debris had been hauled away from the creek. The arborists around here really knew how to cut and run.

Cole popped red candy into his mouth as he assessed the clean-up. A peppery sweetness filled the SUV. "You wouldn't even know we had a storm."

Tomorrow their relationship would vanish like the downed oak limbs. Her heart twinged in her scarred chest. She'd never forget this electrician turned songwriter who saved her life. Tangy cinnamon treats would always remind her of Cole.

"You're right. It's almost all cleaned up," she said casually, as she drove down the lane to Ernie's house.

Ted's brother stood on a ladder as he strung Christmas lights along the porch roof. What if Ernie fell? Poor Gretta was in no condition to drive him to the hospital or lift him from the ground.

"Looks like we arrived just in time." She shifted into park behind Ernie's retro station wagon and Ted's sedan.

Cole set his box of candy on her console and unbuckled his seatbelt. "I'll offer to help but brace yourself for another storm. You've got one stubborn neighbor."

For the time being.

They each grabbed a grocery bag. She gripped the gallon of milk.

"Afternoon, Ernie," she called. Ernie's attention remained riveted on the string of lights. "We brought you some groceries."

Ernie continued his hanging vigil. "I can see that."

Could he? He hadn't turned around or greeted

them. His voice didn't sound thankful.

Cole sauntered toward the ladder. "Want some help? I can feed you the line."

"I've been stringing these lights for years." Ernie shot Cole a glance. "The nails are placed in the exact spot the missus wants them. Except for a few that are missing. You'll mess me up."

How could Ted and Ernie have been raised in the same home? Ted would have thanked Cole for his offer even if he didn't accept it. Gretta was a saint to put up with the grouch.

"Fine." Cole held up his plastic bag. "We'll take the groceries inside." Cole turned toward her and snarled like a T-Rex. She'd never look at the ferocious dinosaur the same way again.

Gretta opened the screen door and hobbled onto the porch before they reached the top of the steps. She rocked side to side in her medical boot. The black straps on her leg accentuated the femininity of her pink cardigan and floral house dress. Her white hair was pulled back in a clip that sparkled.

"Come on in." Her hand swirled with her invite. "You didn't have to bring me anything. We would have made it into town sooner or later." She tilted her head toward Ernie's ladder. "Much later."

"We thought we'd help you out since you provided dinner last night." Sam ducked under Cole's arm as he braced the door open. He removed his baseball cap and followed her into the cozy living room. The indent of the hat made his hair curl at the ends and took several years off of his age. Why couldn't God have sent her a grouchy old man houseguest like Ernie? Then she wouldn't be sad when Cole left.

"It was only hot dogs." Gretta halted before a four-foot Christmas tree, its base swaddled in a red and green quilt and stationed on a tabletop in the corner. The brightness of the lights backlit Gretta, making her an authentic stand-in for Mrs. Claus. "You two are sweet as chess pie. First you clear our trees, and now you bring me some food. I could get used to having you as a neighbor." Gretta winked, her face matching the festive spirit of her decorated tree.

Sam smiled back. "I'll do what I can while I'm here." A shadow of regret about leaving darkened her thoughts. Ted had at least one nephew. Where was Ernie and Gretta's son? Wasn't he concerned about his parents? The *tap, tap, tap* of Ernie's hammering invaded her recollections.

"We actually thought about offering you a Christmas tree." Saved by Cole's admission.

She and Cole put the plastic bags of food on the kitchen table making sure the milk and cold items went into the refrigerator.

Returning to the living room, Cole said, "The storm winds upended two pines that are leaning on Ted's shed. We thought you might like one, but I see you've been busy." He nodded toward the sparkling tree.

Gretta traipsed over to a lounger and sat. "Any other year I would have jumped at the offer. This Christmas, I'm doing as little as possible while I heal.

Here, have a seat." She motioned to two highbacked chairs that faced her recliner.

Sam breathed deep as she settled into the comfy chair. "It sure smells like a real evergreen in here."

"Scented tea light candles." Gretta pointed to a tiny model of a Victorian home sitting on her end table. "A fresh scent and no tree needles to clean up, or watering to be done." Her light-brown penciled eyebrows rose. "And no nagging the husband to do it."

A ringtone interrupted their conversation. It wasn't Sam's phone. Her purse was in the SUV and Gretta wasn't moving to answer a call.

Cole shifted the baseball cap on his thigh and leaned to the side, removing his phone from his pocket. "It's my dad." Cole stared at the display as if it might explode. If she remembered right, Cole and his parents didn't talk much. Had his call yesterday and the news about Ted mended past pain?

"Hello, Dad." Apprehension filled Cole's tone as if he was a teenager explaining the scratches on a new car.

A man's voice, indistinct, reverberated from the phone pushed against Cole's ear.

"When did he go into surgery?" Cole stood. A stunned expression overtook his face as his cap fell to the floor. He strolled toward the screen door and stared outside. "How long ago?"

Sam met Gretta's motherly gaze. "This doesn't sound good," she whispered. Leaning forward, she clasped her hands.

"OK. I'll be there as quick as I can." Cole scrubbed

a hand over his face. When he turned around his features held more shock than when the tornado warning erupted. All the morning's frivolity had escaped his being. "I have to go to Nashville." His eyes slammed shut. "My brother had an accident." A gust of wind rushed from his mouth. "Oh, man. My truck's in the shop."

Gretta scooched to the front of the recliner. "Take Ted's car."

"Ouch!" echoed through the screen door. The nailing of lights halted.

"Are you sure?" Cole's hand trembled as he tried to put his phone in his pocket.

This was lunacy letting him drive in this condition. If anything happened to Cole, she wouldn't forgive herself.

"I appreciate the offer, Gretta, but I'm not sure Cole should be making this drive alone." Sam jumped to her feet, picked Cole's hat off the rug, and grasped his hand. "I'm taking you to Nashville." She used her best don't-talk-back-to-me voice. "We've survived one storm together. What's one more?"

14

Cole eased his seat back as the late afternoon sun blistered I-40 East. Soon, the GPS would have them take the bypass around Nashville. He stretched out his legs, scooting an 'I love my teacher' can coolie to the side of the floor mat. For the last hour, a smooth jazz station attempted to calm his nerves. Sam had said it did wonders for her after an energy charged day at school. He appreciated the small talk and space Sam had given him on the drive. Jillie Lynn would have filled his brain with insider scandals, worst-case scenarios, and copyright controversy. Sam's calm demeanor and encouragement was keeping him sane. He prayed his brother made it through the emergency surgery and recovered fully. *I can do everything through Christ who gives me strength.* Could he be a comfort to his parents if they lost their oldest son? Everything Cole did got lost in his brother's shadow. *Lord, give me strength and wisdom to be what my family needs right now.*

Sam signaled a lane change and checked her rearview mirror. With her sunglasses on and her determined expression, she exuded the confidence of a race car driver. She tilted her head and cast him a glance with a compassionate smile. "We're making good time. Did your dad say how long your brother would be in surgery?"

His dad had been brief. Details were in short supply, as always. He'd cut his dad some slack since his right-hand man and favored son had suffered a terrible collision.

Cole shook his head. "They have to repair a shattered leg. Dad mentioned a broken arm, but I don't think they're doing surgery on it. Wade's lost a lot of blood, so it must have been a bad crash." Cole uncapped a bottle of water and took a swig. His throat grew tight talking about the accident. "My brother was in a company van. If he was in his regular vehicle...I don't want to think about where we would be headed right now." To a funeral home? He chased the image from his mind. Cole replaced the water bottle in the cup holder and offered Sam a drink from her bottle.

"I'll wait. I'd like to get to the hospital without making a pit stop." She forced another half-hearted smile in his direction. "I'm sure your dad would have texted if things weren't going well."

If their family dynamic was normal, maybe, but Cole wasn't sure where he stood after leaving the family business. If anything happened to Wade, his dad would crumble. Wade was the future of Donoven and Son. His brother was the heir, the genius businessman, the strategic planner, the son who always made the correct decisions.

Cole wasn't any of those things. At least, not in his father's eyes or Wade's. Growing up, his dad had been an attentive father. But all that changed when Wade joined the business. His father's goal of making a decent living vaulted to being the number one electrical company in all of Nashville.

"Cole?" Sam faced forward, but with the worry in her voice, she probably side-eyed him from her shades. "Someone would call."

"Yeah, you're right." He sat up straighter feigning confidence. Though in his gut, he knew that if Wade, the brother who received all the accolades passed, Cole, the invisible brother, might get lost in the grieving process.

~*~

The red neon hospital sign declared their arrival. Sam found a parking spot near the front entrance.

Turning to face him, Sam removed her sunglasses. "We should pray together. I've been sending prayers up to God all along the interstate." She reached over the console.

He grasped her soft hands willingly. Her low-key floral perfume energized him like a bird song at the crease of dawn. "I'd like that." He had prayed for Wade, too, but traipsing down Memory Boulevard had clouded his brain. "You first. You're better at this than I am since you had all those years growing up with Ted." He nervously rubbed his thumb on the back of her hand. "Didn't you tell me he was your Sunday school teacher for a while?"

"You can't top that experience. I'll begin." She

bowed her head. "Lord, we lift Wade up to You. Please give the doctors wisdom as they treat his wounds. We pray for a full recovery from surgery. Be with Cole and his parents, Lord. Strengthen them so they can be a comfort to Wade."

Cole would do his best to comfort Wade, but that would mean his brother would have to accept his help. All his life, Cole had tried to follow in his older brother's know-it-all footsteps. Wade had pushed him away.

Pressure seized his hand. His turn to pray.

"God, please heal my brother." He cleared his throat, pushing words through his constricting windpipe. "I don't want to lose him." And he meant it. He loved his brother even though, lately, Wade had been distant. "Be with Mom and Dad during this hard time." His eyes welled with tears. No tears. Not in front of Sam. "In Jesus's name. Amen." He clenched his teeth to keep his composure, and then he let go of Sam's hands. Her warmth lingered on his skin. She had joked that he was her guardian angel. At this moment, her caring nature and bold faith were lifting him closer to God.

Exiting Sam's SUV, they hit the sliding hospital doors at a healthy stride. A blast of chilled air assaulted his senses, masking the odor of disinfectant momentarily.

The receptionist sent him and Sam to the fifth floor. Wade was in critical care recovery and a family waiting room was nearby. The older woman's gaze darted from his face to Sam's as she sternly mentioned the one-family-member visiting policy.

Sam entered the elevator first. She faced the steel doors, her lips firmly set in a thin line. Gone was that cautiously cheerful smile she'd used on him in the car. Was it his imagination? She had mentioned her cancer surgery at their campfire. He didn't recall the length of her treatment or if it was done at a hospital.

He pressed the round fifth floor button. "It hasn't been a boring weekend. You'll have plenty of examples of adversity to use in your classroom."

Her grin returned. "I'm glad I could be with you and get you here safely. If I hadn't offered, I think Ernie would have fallen off of the ladder."

"You heard that thumb strike, too? That eavesdropper is possessive of Ted's car."

Ding. The elevator doors opened. Cole strode out and noticed his dad at the end of the hallway talking to a nurse. His father's shirt was untucked, and his pants appeared to have been left in the dryer for a week.

"Dad." Cole hurried to console his father. Before his dad could flinch or speak, Cole wrapped him in a strong hug. His dad wobbled like a wooden carving. "We came as soon as you called."

"You drove from Ted's?" His dad sniffled and glanced from the nurse to Sam as if he was processing an overload of information.

"Sam drove." Cole indicated his beautiful chauffer. "This is Samantha Williams. A friend of Ted's. And mine." Those two little words at the end of his statement cradled his heart. He didn't know what he would have done if Sam hadn't offered to accompany him. Would he be pacing the tile flooring in reception?

The nurse excused herself with some assurances that she would monitor Wade's condition.

Ever the comforter, Sam rested a hand on his dad's arm. "We've been praying for Wade."

"Thank you. I appreciate your help." His dad's head bobbed. "Your mom went to grab a bite in the cafeteria. We've been here since the police called." Rubbing his forehead as though he needed some caffeine and food, his dad said, "I was going to sit with Wade, but you should see him."

Cole was fairly sure that Wade would prefer their father's company. "Sure, I'll see him." *Lord, don't let this be the last time.*

Sam hugged her purse to her chest and rotated her shoulders. "I'll find the cafeteria and some snacks. I'll keep praying." Her hazel eyes bored into Cole. "Text me if you need something. Anything. Only one person is allowed in, and you don't need me now." She excused herself with kind words to his father.

How wrong she was about needing her. "OK. I'll find you," Cole said. That elusive lump lodged in his throat. Up until now, he could worry, castigate, ache, regret, pray, and pretend to be someone he was not. He wasn't a carefree lumberjack or a lifesaver who role-played with kids and charmed elderly neighbors. Walking into the recovery ward, he was the little brother that Wade never wanted.

~*~

Cole rushed toward the third curtained room trying not to disturb any of the other patients. He hardly recognized Wade. His brother's head was bandaged, and his eyes were puffy. Small cuts covered his face. The black casting on his arm reminded Cole of Gretta's foot contraption. Wade's right leg was suspended by a pulley. Being a tall guy, Wade's covers barely made it to his lower chest. Cole had never seen his brother so savagely injured.

A nurse punched buttons on a vital-signs monitor while the hum of a blood pressure cuff awakened the silence.

"Good. Your blood pressure is coming down nicely, Mr. Donoven." The nurse checked the IV bag and rounded the bed. "I'll be back shortly. Her demeanor screamed "make it quick."

Wade turned ever so slightly toward Cole. A long groan erupted from his lips. "Now I know I'm dying. The baby of the family has arrived." Wade's mouth curved into a smile and abruptly flattened.

Cole's brain emptied of a response or conversation. Think like Sam. "I, uh…I've been praying for you."

Letting out a sigh, his brother nestled into the pillow. "Right." He closed his eyes as if dismissing his visitor. "You worked customer emergencies on Sunday. I should have been home on my couch." His eyes slowly opened. "I'm surprised you're here."

"Dad called." That was more of a logistical answer. "You're my brother. Only one, last time I checked."

Wade stared at him, half-lidded, with his mother's gray-blue eyes. "Did you bring the stripper?"

And this was why they weren't close. Cole fisted his hand as heat consumed his neck. He stifled a rebuttal. Wade had always found fault in Cole's work and choices.

His brother winced, swore, and then muttered about broken ribs.

The rise and fall of Wade's heartbeat on the monitor, the blood seeping through the gauze, Wade being immobile in a bed, didn't seem real. It was surreal, and frightening, and Cole didn't know how to make it better. *Be compassionate.* "Would you like me to get the nurse?" Cole's gaze settled on the bed table by the monitor. "How about something to drink?"

"Ice chips." Wade's features collapsed into a myriad of wrinkles. "I need you to step up."

Cole raced into action and held the cup to his brother's lips. "Is that enough?"

Wade crunched a little ice. "No." He closed his eyes while his breathing slowed. "I'm supposed to meet investors in Sperry's Crossing. It's down to two bids. I've got the blueprints and figures on a flash drive. Dad's too overwhelmed, so you've got to help him."

Standing above his brother's bed with the cold of the ice penetrating his fingers, Cole finally understood about Sperry's Crossing. The industrial park being built out by Whispering Creek. His dad had mentioned that Wade was bidding on work there. Work Cole knew nothing about. He hadn't been an employee of the family business for almost three years, and now Wade wanted him to act like the company president.

Cole set the ice chip cup on the side table and stroked the back of his neck. The chill of his fingers confirmed this wasn't a dream. "I'll go get, Dad." Cole backed around the bed. "We'll talk later."

Wade's eyes closed as Cole hurried out of the recovery room and into the hallway. *I can do everything through Christ who gives me strength.*

Tipping his head toward the marbled ceiling tiles, Cole whispered, "Lord, I get it, but I don't know the first thing about what Wade proposed. Am I supposed to dive into blueprints and staffing plans when I've got a song to write?" His brother was the visionary strategic planner. Cole fixed outlets and fuse boxes. He braced his hands on his hips. "I'm not Wade Donoven," he mumbled.

One of the verses he had read in the morning played in his mind. *Do not be anxious about anything.*

"Well, God, it's a little late for that."

15

Sam pushed the lobby button and collapsed against the side of the elevator. Her body temperature was tropical, but a hand to her forehead didn't indicate a fever. Memories of all her doctor visits, needle pokes, and surgeries came to life in her brain. She hated hospitals, and she wasn't done with surgery, not if she wanted to reconstruct her right breast. She breathed deep and exhaled, adjusting her prosthetic before the elevator door opened. *Get a grip.* Wade was the one in recovery, not her, at least, not now.

As she strolled toward the reception desk, a reality check emboldened her spirits. Next time, she would go under the knife on her timetable; soon, down the road, or never. All she had to worry about was fixing her house and getting home for Christmas. Somehow the damage to her window and porch weren't as frustrating after hearing about Wade's accident. She and Cole had survived a storm without a scratch. Wade's life had been upended on a Sunday afternoon drive. *Lord, help me be strong for Cole and his family. Please heal Wade fully from this trauma.*

The lady at the welcome desk pointed her in the direction of the cafeteria. Most of the tables were empty except for a few people in scrubs. A cashier waited in front of a take-out refrigerator as most of the kitchen was dark and without a chef or server in sight. Even hospital cafeteria workers needed a rest at 6:45 PM on a Sunday. Sam grabbed a few sandwiches and drinks and paid the cashier whose coral jacket reminded her of Gretta.

Why hadn't Ernie and Gretta's son come to check on them after the storm? He could have strung Christmas lights. Was that why Ted had left her his house, so she could help his family? Ted had gone on and on about the mild winters in Tennessee, trying to coax her parents into buying property nearby. A visit to Whispering Creek was postponed by her diagnosis and surgery, but God's timing was perfect. Maybe she needed to be in Tennessee now.

Rejoice in the Lord always. She didn't rejoice in Ted's passing, but she rejoiced knowing Ted had a mansion in heaven that was storm proof.

She carried her bag of food to a table and noticed a woman sitting alone picking at her sandwich. If by some prearranged cue, the dark-haired woman glanced at Sam. Those were the same eyes and nose as her houseguest. A cool shiver washed over Sam. If the woman wasn't Cole's mom, then a DNA swab was justified. Should she ask? Better to introduce herself and be dismissed than to explain a snub if they met later on.

Walking toward the table, Sam gave what she hoped was a comforting smile. "Mrs. Donoven?"

The woman's eyes widened. Her alert meter skyrocketed.

"I'm Samantha Williams." Sam gauged if she had made the right call. "I'm a friend of Ted Beckman's and …"

"Cole's here?" The woman stood and waved for Sam to join her.

"I think Cole is seeing Wade as we speak. We came as soon as your husband called. Cole was shaken up, so I drove. His truck's in the shop." Sam settled her purse and plastic food bag on the table.

"I'm so glad you came over. Have a seat. And please call me Linda." Tears glistened in Linda's eyes as she sat. "I didn't know if Cole would come. I've been praying." Linda leaned back in her chair, her upper body relaxing a bit. She dabbed at her eye with a crumpled napkin. "I don't know how two brothers could be so different. I was hoping something would bring them together. I certainly didn't expect this."

Sam laid a gentle hand on Linda's shoulder, recognizing that look of helplessness etched in a mother's face. Her own cancer diagnosis had turned her mother's complexion ashen and drawn. "I'm so sorry. We prayed for Wade on our way here."

"You did? Cole, too?" A glimpse of relief brightened Linda's features.

Sam nodded. "Cole prayed. He's got a big heart." Sam's belly blossomed with memories of Cole's strong arms whisking her to safety and all the labor he had done to help Ernie.

"Cole always has." Linda sniffled. "I wish his brother would have appreciated it. Wade liked being an only child. He forged ahead with life and left his little brother to fend for himself." Linda's thick-lashed eyes blinked back another infantry of tears. "Do you have siblings?"

Sam shook her head and unwrapped her sandwich. "I'm an only child. But I have a friend, Emma, who is like a sister to me. We're close, and we don't have to share parents." She grinned even though soggy lettuce and bland mayonnaise soured her tastebuds.

Linda cupped a hand over her mouth as she chewed her sandwich. "I pray one day my boys will realize what a blessing it is to have a brother."

Cole seemed to come out of nowhere and grip his mom's chair. "What? Wade's blessed to have me as a brother?" He flashed his charming grin. "I see you met Sam."

Linda leapt from her seat and hugged her son.

Sam wished her mother was here to hug. Witnessing Cole and his mother's embrace caressed her weary heart. She wouldn't mind being bear-hugged in Cole's capable arms either. She had seen Cole at his worst and at his best and everything in-between. The honest emotions they had shared in the past two days had her affections tied in a craft store bow. But she had held back sharing one loss. A loss she didn't know how to share with a man who made her think beyond Monday and left her yearning for another intimate campfire.

Cole wedged a chair between them. "Wade's feeling better. He wants to put me to work meeting investors at Sperry's Crossing."

Linda rested an arm on the back of Cole's seat. "You don't have to do it, son. There will be other projects, and the timing will be better."

"I know." Cole shot Sam a glance as if they shared a secret code. He cracked a smile, and then scanned the ceiling briefly before reengaging with his mother. "I've been thinking that maybe God had a reason for sending me out to Whispering Creek."

Talk about a power punch. Cole was bringing up God and giving her an endearing smile at the same time. A parade of butterflies encircled her heart.

Cole stroked his stubbled chin. "I mean, I went to visit Ted, and I met Sam. At the moment, I'm stranded in Whispering Creek. My truck's in the shop there." His pensive grin widened. "I'm out near the new industrial complex that Wade was teed up to visit on Thursday. That can't all be coincidence. Am I missing something spiritual?"

Had she been so focused on her problems that she had missed God's plan as well? Cole was right about being skeptical about all the coincidences. She had heard a sermon about divine appointments. Had God brought her to Whispering Creek at this moment for a purpose? God didn't sit up in the heavens watching the world spin. God was involved in the details of her life, actively involved.

Ted was one of the wisest men she knew, a man of prayer, and he had seen fit to leave her his home. He also had taught her that joy started with a J. And that the J stood for Jesus. Had she taken her eyes off of Jesus and focused too much on worldly concerns? She should enjoy each day and not be anxious about next week. Her window, shingles, and porch would get fixed eventually. As would her body.

Her phoned buzzed in her purse. She discreetly checked the message as Cole and his mom talked.

Emma texted: *Are you ignoring me? Or are you and Cowboy Cole hitting the town now that ur sprung? Smiley face. Red heart.*

If Emma only knew about their race to the hospital. But it looked as though Cole would be in Whispering Creek a while longer, and she was determined to enjoy every day with him. In Sam's eyes that was a huge smiley face.

16

Cole rubbed his eyes. How long had he been staring at his dad's desktop? Long enough to see why Wade didn't want to punt on the bid. The electrical engineer for the developer knew his stuff, and Wade had matched the engineer's mindset with exceptional detail and reasoning. Cole disagreed with the original engineer on one fuse box placement, but it was nothing to sink a bid over. Plopping another spicy cheese puff into his mouth, he checked his phone: 8:52 AM. His mother would be returning from the hospital soon. His parents were tag teaming to keep Wade company. He'd help as much as he could before returning to Whispering Creek. He needed his truck fixed and to sell his brother's proposal to investors in the industrial park.

A few thunks sounded from the hallway. Sam had been given permission to go through his closet for old toys and collectibles that she could use in her classroom. He didn't realize his mom hadn't cleared out the games and toys years ago. Too bad Sam didn't have a teaching position in Whispering Creek. She was becoming a good friend. The kind who always had your back and thought ahead to the future. Sam had the wisdom to pack some overnight clothes. She was also the reason they had stayed at his childhood home.

He couldn't take her to his one-bedroom apartment. And if they had left, he wouldn't have walked in on Sam praying with his dad this morning over pancakes. His boyhood home actually felt like home again with Sam around. He hoped she stayed in Whispering Creek because he didn't want to see her taillights heading north.

Sam strolled through the living room carrying a large plastic tub. She halted at the office door and set down her treasure chest. Her gorgeous smile was like jumper cables to his heart.

"If I had known you had flash cards, an unopened board game, and every species of toy dinosaur, I would have invited myself over earlier."

He chuckled at her enthusiasm over his junk. "I'm glad my hand-me-downs are bringing you so much joy."

"You were holding out on me." She picked up a dinosaur figurine from the tub. "Look at this T-Rex. Daniel would love it. No wonder you were such an authentic growler."

"You mean my roars." He rolled the office chair away from the desk and grasped the T-Rex. "This might have been Wade's, but he owes me for saving his bid. We can bring it to Daniel when we take the Christmas tree over. That is, if Lucinda hasn't put one up since we've been here."

"I doubt it." Sam secured her hair behind her ear. "Last time we saw Lucinda, she was swamped. Who knows if her mom is back on her feet? Daniel still may be roaring at customers." Sam reclaimed the dinosaur and placed it back in the tub. The touch of her soft skin lingered on his hand. "You're sure you don't mind me taking these toys? You could keep a few."

"For what? To gather dust?"

"You might have kids someday. They don't make models like they used to."

Months ago, he wouldn't have had a conversation about children. Jillie Lynn avoided kids, babies, or even sitting anywhere near a family. With Sam, the talk of kids was commonplace. She'd spent years studying how to teach them. He could see her patiently helping a child with homework or dressed up in a silly costume to entertain her class.

"It's fine." He waved off her concern. "I bet Wade's closet is full of toys, too. If I get desperate, I'll borrow some of his. Although, I have to say, I had cooler toys."

"Speaking of your brother." Sam leaned over the side of the desk and squinted at the diagram on the screen. "How's the presentation looking? It's been too quiet since your dad left."

The scent of Sam's body wash filled the office area and jolted his awareness of her. She looked as though she was back in college with her team hoodie, and they were having a study date. He and Sam had done a lot together, though he wouldn't call the activities a date. He needed to change that fact and stop daydreaming.

He swiveled in the office chair. "I'm impressed with Wade's work. He's put a lot of time into these plans. There's only one part of the original blueprint that I would change. It's out of my pay grade."

"Doesn't hurt to have a backup plan. Or an extra credit assignment." She crossed her arms, bunching the oversized fleece. "Do you miss being an electrician? After all, your first save at Ted's house was fixing my lights."

"True, but that wasn't as heroic as my scoop and dump in the tub." He flexed his bicep as she shook her head in mock disbelief.

"I'm being serious." She sure didn't look that way standing next to a bin of toys and resembling an undergrad.

Did he miss being part of the family business? Deep down, yes, but there was more to his leaving than being bored of rewiring outlets and replacing fixtures. He rose and headed to the closet in his dad's office. When he slid the closet door open, a slight waft of freshly sewn hats filled his nostrils. He grabbed a baseball cap from hundreds stacked in a box. He tossed it toward Sam. "Heads up."

She caught the cap one-handed and read the embroidery. "Ooh, now I'm official. Donoven and Sons Electric." She shoved the cap over her hair and tucked wayward strands under the rim.

"Minus one for the teacher."

"What?" Her excitement waned a notch. He was calling out the teacher.

"It's Donoven and Son Electric." He emphasized the sole heir and pointed to the wording on the hat. "My dad never made it plural. Even after my first year of service. Some of the guys used to tease me that I was the black sheep of the family. Or worse, that I wasn't legit."

"That's awful. Did you ever ask your dad about it?"

Should he have? *What a whiner* is what his brother used to say when he tattled to his parents about Wade riding off on his bike and leaving him stranded. He figured his dad didn't think he was as serious about the business as Wade. The company seemed like a video game contest where there were only two controllers, and he was the odd man out. Father and eldest son had everything running fine. It pained his ego that he was invisible to his dad.

"I never asked my dad about it." He crossed his arms and leaned against the far side of the desk trying to hide the hurt that his own family didn't think he was sharp enough to run the business. "It made it easier to leave. The name of the company didn't have to be changed from sons back to son."

Sam slouched in the office chair and strummed her fingers on the armrest. "And I thought I missed out on not having a brother or a sister. I never had to compete for my parent's attention or deal with a bossy sister. I guess we'll have to pray that God lets you know where He wants you to use your gifts." She swiveled in the chair and stopped so her gaze met his. "You have lots of talents. More than most people I know. You can write songs, play the guitar, and figure out how to wire buildings. Plus…" She pointed a finger at him with such dramatic empathy that he forgot for a moment what he had revealed. "You can imitate a T-Rex and charm an energetic boy. You have a multitude of skills."

"Do I? I've never made a list." Hearing Sam speak about his talents made his cheeks sizzle hotter than his flaming snack.

Maybe God was giving him something to focus on other than one last song with Jillie Lynn. He had options. No one was forcing him to choose music over the family business. Work at Donoven and Son would be plentiful if he secured the bid. And he needed to get right with God. Sam possessed spiritual skills that Cole was rusty at. Such as what he'd witnessed in the kitchen. He placed a hand on the highbacked chair and shifted it so all Sam could see was him.

"Hey, thanks for praying with my dad this morning." Saying the words created a lump in his throat. "I'm sure he enjoyed your company and support. Dynamite couldn't have blasted my mom from Wade's bedside."

"Your parents are great." She smiled, stood, and sauntered toward a wall of family pictures. "This house reminds me of my home in Wisconsin."

"Really? Your mom likes country blues and ducks?" He joined her in scrutinizing the family pictures from over the decades. He was pretty sure he could slip a picture of Sam on the wall, and she would fit right in.

"My mom is more the country cabin type. But I can feel that this house holds a lot of love."

His parents loved him. But the last few years had been strained. That was partly his fault in not overriding his girlfriend and her diss on religion or anyone who couldn't further her career. Sam had brought back the excitement of being part of a family. She'd also brought the peace of God with her. The same peace Cole had felt at Ted's place.

Do not be anxious about anything.

Strange how he wasn't afraid about finishing one more song or presenting his brother's proposal. The thing that scared him the most was that Sam would drive away, back to Wisconsin, and leave tire tracks all over his heart.

~*~

Cole poked his head into Wade's hospital room. His dad rested in a recliner in the corner, a magazine balanced on his leg. Wade was still slung like a hammock with his leg elevated.

Wade stirred when Cole approached the bed. The peaks and valleys on Wade's heart monitor sped.

"I thought you'd be long gone." His brother's voice sounded rough.

"You gave me too much work to do. I've been studying all morning." At the moment, Cole was studying his cowboy boots against the tiled floor.

"So, you're going to help us out and pitch the bid Thursday?" Cole wasn't sure if the 'us' included him, or if Wade was possessive of the two-Donoven business model.

"Someone's got to save your backside." Cole grinned, but not too big. His brother was irate about being stuck at the hospital. *Encourage him like Sam would.* "You did nice work on that bid." He shrugged. "Besides, I don't mind staying out by Whispering Creek."

"Mom says you have a new girlfriend." Always like Wade to drop a hook and go fishing. Well, his brother would have to wait on specifics. Cole didn't have everything figured out yet.

"She's a friend. Time will tell where it leads."

"Win the bid and you can see her often enough." Wade tried to shift higher on the bed.

Cole rearranged his brother's pillows. Wade wouldn't ask for help. Not from his little brother. For years, Cole had been waiting for his big brother to reach out and invite him into the inner circle of the business. Wade never flinched. Maybe this accident was a way for Cole to show his brother how much he cared. On Wade's terms. Clearing his throat, Cole said, "If she stays and doesn't race back to Wisconsin, I'll be in close proximity."

Wade's head burrowed deeper into his fluffed pillows. "Give her a reason to stay."

Cole laughed. "Spoken by a man who hasn't dated seriously in years."

"I'm waiting for the perfect Mrs. Donoven." Wade grinned, but Cole suspected the euphoria was because of his pain meds.

"I've got the perfect Mrs. Donoven and don't you boys forget it." His dad opened the holiday living magazine.

"Score one for dad." Cole edged closer to his

brother careful not to bump his body. "I'm praying for your healing, bro." And he was, thanks to Sam's influence and God's grace.

Wade's eye widened. "You're full of surprises, little brother."

God was full of surprises. All Cole had planned was to have a quiet weekend at Ted's unofficial Bed and Breakfast. The weekend had come and gone, and it had been anything but quiet. Monday rolled around, and he was comforting a brother he hadn't talked to in years, and he offered to pray for him to get better. A family emergency storm had changed the course of his future, the second storm in three days that had upended his life. He glanced at his dad and brother. His chest felt lighter as if a few cinder blocks had fallen off the wall protecting his pride. *Lord, I don't know if I can handle another storm.*

Cole rubbed his forehead. "Yes, I guess I am changing things up a bit." He stifled a contemplative grin. "I also borrowed your blue suit for the pitch."

17

An open parking spot waited not far from A Brew 4 You. Sam had given the keys to her SUV to Cole since driving with a Christmas tree on the roof was not in her skill set. The festive wreaths on the lampposts twinkled in the dark sky. Six o'clock might as well have been midnight on this Tuesday night.

Sam had called and told Lucinda about the free tree. The café owner was ecstatic. Lucinda suggested they arrive when her last remaining customers could witness the fun and Daniel would have an hour to wind down before the café closed.

After exiting the car, Cole untied the pine and grabbed the trunk of the tree. His handsome face was lost in a sea of branches.

"Would you like to grasp the tip and help guide this sucker off your car?"

Sam pulled on her gloves. She already had enough sticky sap on her flannel shirt to make her smell like Gretta's Christmas-scented tealights.

"Are you kidding? After the insurance adjuster told me I only have to pay a deductible and they'll fix my house, I bet I could race this puppy inside all by myself." She had been thanking God all afternoon for the news. The money Ted had left would cover her deductible. Ted couldn't have known a storm would hit so soon after his death, but she couldn't help thinking he was watching out for her.

She looped a bag over her arm that held Cole's boyhood T-Rex and grabbed the thinning trunk of the tip of the tree. Cole bore the brunt of the pine's weight as he removed their gift from the top of her car.

"I think I got the raw end of the deal." Cole caught his breath after bracing the base of the trunk on the asphalt.

"Well, you wanted the heavy part." She rested her gloves on her hips, happy they had an open parking spot next to the SUV. Cole shook his head, but he looked pleased to play a lumberjack. One didn't get to wrestle a tree every day, although lately Cole had slain a lot of oaks.

"That's not what I meant. I think I paid as much for my truck's deductible as you did for the deductible on the house."

"Single, twenty-something male. Don't you have the worst driving records?" She laughed as he pulled a sad face.

"Come on, single, twenty-something female." He nodded toward the storefront. "I think I see Daniel fogging up the front window. I'll come back for my guitar."

Lucinda opened the front door. Christmas bells jingled as she gently maneuvered Daniel away from the opening.

Sam threaded the tip of the tree through the doorway. "Merry Christmas."

~*~

"I help," Daniel said. He grabbed a single branch close to Cole's position. The boy grunted a few times as Cole carried the weight of the tree and maneuvered it toward the far corner of the cafe without injuring any customers.

She kept the tree upright while Cole secured it in the base. Her rugged new friend was a welcomed gift. The past few days had been a challenge, but she and Cole had focused on God, and somehow the chaos didn't seem so chaotic. She breathed in the scent of evergreen and freshly brewed coffee. This had to be what heaven smelled like.

Lucinda carried a box of Christmas decorations and set it on a table closest to the tree. "Everything should be fairly new." She gestured toward two older ladies at the register. "You don't mind if I leave you for a little while?"

"We've got this." Sam motioned toward the customers. "One preschooler is a breeze for me."

"You're my hero," Lucinda whispered.

Sam set the T-Rex bag near an empty table for later and stretched the green plastic wires securing the lights. She plugged them into an outlet to make sure they worked. Daniel squatted and stared at the lights. The tiny bulbs reminded Sam of glistening snow. Her blood must have thinned being in Tennessee. Fifty degrees was becoming her go-to temperature for winter.

"Why don't you help me feed the strings to Cole?"

She unplugged the lights. "We don't want them to tangle."

"OK. Me and Co do it." Daniel held out his hands, moving the string of bulbs as if they were precious newborns.

Her heart blossomed. She missed teaching a room full of kids. Christmas was fun and festive and full of meaning. Jesus was the light of the world. How many lesson plans had she written with Jesus being the lights on the tree or how a star had shown the wise men where to find the toddler Jesus. She'd even wrapped a gift with Jesus's name inside. Hopefully, she would have her own classroom next year. Either here, or in Wisconsin. Her inherited property was starting to feel like home.

When Cole and Daniel had finished stringing the tiny bulbs, Daniel held his arms open. "See Sam?"

She beamed brighter than the little lights. She had made friends in this small Tennessee town.

"Good job, honey. You and your mom are going to have the prettiest tree."

"Hey, what about me?" Cole flexed in his camo hoodie. "I studied all day."

"Good job, 'oney." Daniel giggled and did a happy dance in front of the tree.

Cole pretended to sulk.

She tamped down her smile. Many a customer hid their enjoyment behind a coffee mug.

Cole held her keys high. "I'll bring in my guitar. You can decorate while I play some songs."

"Now, that's a deal. I'm behind on listening to

Christmas music this season." She chose red-frosted bulbs and a box of candy canes to start decorating the tree. The candy canes could be hung in the shape of a J for Jesus. Oh, how she missed being in a classroom during December.

She decorated the tree, top bulbs for her, lower bulbs for Daniel.

Cole returned and strummed "We Wish You a Merry Christmas."

Sam wasn't an expert on guitar skills, but Cole played with ease. He didn't even balk when a guy requested "Jingle Bells."

"Here's one for Wisconsin Sam." Cole started strumming "White Christmas."

She pulled over a chair and listened to Cole's serenade. Daniel climbed onto her lap. The boy's gaze never left Cole's fingers as Cole changed chords. Daniel relaxed against her chest when Cole went into "Tennessee Christmas." Of course, he'd play that song. Aren't you supposed to know your audience? Or was it a subtle mind game?

Daniel shifted, squirmed, and shifted some more. Had he felt her prosthetic? She had almost forgotten about the soft-plastic bump on her chest. The boy turned in her lap and crinkled his nose. The guitar didn't hold his interest. Uh oh, he wouldn't? Before she could move Daniel off of her lap, he tapped her fake boob. Once. Twice. Before she could hold his wrist, he palmed her prosthetic like it was being scolded for not being a good enough head rest. Her breast flattened like a squishy toy.

Heart rate spiking as her face grew warm, she glanced around to see how many people saw her chest shift. Customers spoke intently with gazes darting her direction. There were witnesses, but they weren't her main concern.

She gently grasped Daniel's hand. "We don't touch people in private places. We need to ask permission to come into someone's personal space." She looped a hand in front of her chest.

Cole stopped strumming, which made the situation worse.

Everyone stared at Cole, Daniel, and her.

Daniel cocked his head, obviously still trying to figure out the weirdness of her chest.

"You have a hard lump." Daniel's index finger squiggled like a worm toward her prosthetic.

Lucinda rushed over. She mirrored a teen watching a horror movie. "I am so sorry." She scolded Daniel to keep his hands to himself.

Sam didn't want to see Daniel humiliated. "I talked to Daniel." Her whole body flamed and not from the two adults suddenly surrounding her and one fearful boy slumped in her lap. Her secret had been outed by curious fingers, and now she had some serious stuff to explain to a preschooler, and more importantly to Cole.

"I'm not like everyone else. My chest felt different against Daniel's head." She glanced at Cole and Lucinda, but the one who really needed an explanation was the scared child in her lap. She could handle this. Although, nothing like this situation had come up on her final exams.

Bending her head closer to Daniel, she addressed her lap-sitter. She could do this. Explain cancer to a kid. "Daniel, do you know what cancer is?" The "c" word warbled a little.

The boy shook his head.

Daniel was her sole focus. She blocked the adults from her brain and addressed the boy as if they were the only two people sitting by the Christmas tree.

"Cancer is like a sickness. It makes your body sick."

Rubbing his hands together, Daniel said, "I sick with a cold."

"I'm sure you felt bad when your nose got runny. Cancer is like a T-Rex of a cold, but it doesn't go away on its own. In fact, the doctor has to remove it like a wart or a blister." Cole was probably sprinting toward the door. She reached for the plastic bag holding the hand-me-down dinosaur laying by her chair. "Do you know what this dinosaur figurine is made of?"

"Plas-ic." Daniel reached for her illustration, but she shifted it away. The original owner of the dinosaur had put his guitar in its case and angled to hear her every word.

Sam hugged her little friend tighter. "Yes, plastic. You are such a smart boy and that is why you knew there was something different when you leaned against me. I had cancer right here." She rotated her dinosaur-clutching hand over her prosthetic that had thankfully popped into a normal shape.

"You had cancer?" Daniel's voice rose as if she

was somehow special in having the T-Rex disease.

"I did. And when the doctor removed it from my body. I was lopsided, so he made a plastic bump for me to wear. That's what your head hit when you sat in my lap. And we don't touch people in private places even if they feel like a big, plastic, brontosaurus," she whispered. "Do you understand?"

Daniel nodded. "You got T-Rex plas-ic for your bump."

"Yes, I do." Sam laughed and hugged Daniel. "And this T-Rex is for you. Straight from Cole's boyhood home."

Daniel jumped out of her lap and held the dinosaur high. A roar erupted from his mouth.

Cole strolled toward Daniel.

Lucinda crouched by Sam's chair. "You're OK now, aren't you? No more cancer?" Tears glistened in Lucinda's eyes.

Sam wrestled her own tears. This was supposed to be a fun night. Not a breast cancer discussion. "Praise the Lord, I am cancer-free."

"I'm so sorry that you had to go through all of that, Sam." Lucinda swiped wetness from her cheek. "You have been such a good friend to me and Daniel."

Rising, Sam hugged the teary-eyed brunette. Lucinda held on tight even after all the cancer talk. "You and Daniel make Whispering Creek feel like home." Sam pulled away and cleared her throat. "I could use a cinnamon roll and some hot chocolate after I get a breath of fresh air."

"I'll make that a double." Lucinda nodded toward

Cole who was interacting with Daniel. She hurried toward the confections case while checking on customers.

Sam glanced at Cole. He had Daniel wrapped in a bear hug and was lifting the boy and his dinosaur off the floor. With Cole occupied, she could get outside and gather her composure.

Pushing open the door to the café, Sam ignored the jingling bells, and sucked in the cool night air. The crispness of the December night had her casting off classroom mode and embracing the reality of a young woman with a scarred chest. She took a few steps and heard the ding-a-ling of Lucinda's front door. She cringed.

"Don't get in your car and drive away." Cole sauntered beside her swaying as if they were two childhood besties.

"I can't. You have the keys." She forced herself to look into his mesmerizing eyes. Why did her houseguest have to be so cute? She took a few more steps and plopped on a bench outside of Benedictine's Hardware. Garland decorated with red and green tools framed the window. Slouching, she covered her face with her hands. *I am such a freak.*

Cole sat beside her, jostling her leg. Was he trying to get her to look at him?

She dropped her hands into her lap. "I'm sorry."

"For what?" Cole scrubbed a hand through his hair dislodging a few pieces of glitter from Lucinda's decorations. "I think you deserve a sticker for what happened in there."

It wouldn't have been so humiliating if she had told Cole about her botched surgery at the bonfire. "I should have told you about my prosthetic when I mentioned the cancer."

"Really, I don't know if I would have told someone I had just met that I was missing...body parts." Cole grasped her hand and leaned closer. She prayed he wouldn't kiss her because she wanted to forget the past fifteen minutes of her life and a kiss from Cole would hold nothing but pity. "You trusted me with your cancer diagnosis and surgery. That was brave." He squeezed her hand and the tingles traveling the length of her arm were fogging some of the night's horrors. "I'm sorry someone as nice as you had to deal with cancer."

A tear leaked from her eye. She swept the wetness away with the hand that wasn't attached to Cole. "Let's not say I'm sorry again tonight."

"You're right. We're celebrating the Christmas spirit." Cole beheld her as if they were still singing joyous songs. "And you're an early gift." He intertwined their fingers as if he was never letting go. If only she could allow her heart to believe that truth when her secret had scandalized an entire café.

"Well then, God did a gift exchange because you already saved my life once and you pretty near saved it again tonight." She smiled to bring the fun and festivity back into their evening and to banish talk of her deformity. "Oh, I ordered hot chocolate and cinnamon rolls before leaving the café. I think..."

"Lucinda has some sriracha sauce?" He let go of

her hand and tapped his chin.

"You wouldn't put that on a cinnamon roll?"

Cole shook his head. "I was thinking I'd drip some in the hot chocolate." The most delightfully impish expression covered Cole's face. "It'll keep my mouth warm."

Her insides flamed hotter than the sriracha as she envisioned kissing Cole. "Then we better get going because the café closes in twenty minutes."

He stood, helped her to her feet, and reclaimed her hand. A small gesture of whatever relationship had begun between them, but she couldn't help feeling he'd leave her in the dust once his truck was fixed. He swung her arm as if they were a couple, and as if having a girlfriend with only one breast wasn't a big deal. It had been a dealbreaker before. But Cole offered her more support in one night than Karlton had in months.

Cole opened the door to Lucinda's café. "After you."

She scanned the room and contemplated fleeing from the restaurant. One or two people stared at her and Cole. Their smiles held only a hint of sympathy.

Daniel crouched by the sparkling Christmas tree gently touching Cole's guitar. His head jerked, and he came charging toward her.

"Sam." Daniel grabbed her hand. "I watch your food."

On the table where she had revealed why she had a hard bump on her chest, rested two mugs of hot chocolate and two cinnamon rolls.

She and Cole sat, and Daniel joined them, dragging his chair closer to her.

"I like you, Sam," Daniel said on a long breath that made it seem as if he had been doing hard labor while they were gone.

"I like Sam, too, Buddy." Cole held out his fist to Daniel for a bump, and Daniel obliged.

A piece of cinnamon roll nearly caught in her mouth. She sipped her hot chocolate and studied Cole whose smile was vintage Donoven. Did Cole like her as a trusted friend who happened to be a girl, or more of a significant other? Or was she stuck in-between?

"There's a whole lot of like at this table, Daniel." At least in her heart. She grinned at her two dark-haired guys. "I'm happy that Cole and I have a new friend."

Daniel raised his hand-me-down, plas-ic dinosaur and roared.

Rejoice in the Lord. Always.

Maybe this night could be saved after all.

18

Cole made small talk while Sam drove to Ted's. Should he bring up the prosthetic and reassure her that she looked healthy and great? Or would the earlier embarrassment be brought to mind? He was out of his league discussing breast surgery. Their day had started at a hospital and then Sam had to explain cancer to a child. The day couldn't end on another downer. He wanted to convince Sam that she'd be happy settling down in Whispering Creek.

As Sam parked her SUV in front of the porch, he rotated in his seat and readied his persuasive charm. Sam's usual perky vibe had been lost along the county road. He would lure her vibrant smile out of hiding and bask in its brightness. Nothing amped him up more than Sam smiling.

"How about we take the UTV out tonight? We could drive up the hill and look at the stars. I could use some fresh air." *And I bet you could too.* He rubbed his hands together trying to energize the atmosphere in the front seat.

Sam's lips pressed tight. She glanced his direction. "Don't you have to study Wade's proposal?"

Her teacher mode was bubbling below the surface. Homework first. He rested a hand on her arm so she wouldn't bolt for the house.

She shimmied closer into his touch. A good sign.

"I studied earlier today, and there's always tomorrow. It's electricity. It's static."

"Oh, that's bad." Her laugh and smile jolted his heart rate. Score! She crinkled her nose. "What about Ernie? He's pretty possessive of his land."

She was not getting off of his hook. "We'll drive over and let him know we're going for a ride. Gretta will keep him in line." Cole hopped out of the SUV and dipped his head inside to seal the deal. Her flowery perfume and the faint scent of cinnamon accelerated his sales pitch. "Come on. Grab a jacket, and I'll fire up the UTV." *Help me here, Lord.*

Leaning back against the headrest, Sam cracked a grin. "How can a girl resist an offer from a guy who makes jokes about electricity?" Sam exited the car. "I'll grab my jacket. I didn't dress to go hunting."

Cole had in more ways than one. He started the UTV and picked up Sam by the front walkway. She was all smiles on the drive over to Ernie's house. *Thank You, Lord.*

They couldn't miss Ernie's modest home with the beacon of icicle lights. The crisp, ashy scent of a fireplace made the night air wrap around Cole like a fleece vest. As he shut off the vehicle, Ernie opened the door.

"It's a little late for a visit." The old man stood guard in the doorway. His hospitality still needed work.

"Ernest, ask Cole how his brother's doing."

Gretta's voice filtered through the screened door.

"Wade's doing as good as can be expected, Gretta." Cole raised his voice so that it carried through the threshold. "We visited him in Nashville this morning and made it back into town. Thanks for asking." Cole would never understand how that woman married Ernie.

"We're not here for a visit though," Sam called from the passenger seat. Peacemaker Sam was at it again. "We're going stargazing and didn't want you to worry if you heard the motor."

Or get out your shotgun.

"Stargazing, huh?" Ernie shifted the ball cap on his head. "Is that what they call it these days?" He snickered. "Hey Gretta, let's go look at the stars." Ernie performed a few stilted dance moves. Cole worried that Ernie would dislodge a hip.

"Leave the kids alone and close the door. Have fun kids," Gretta said from the living room.

"That's our cue to get out of here." Cole fired the UTV into life again.

Sam snorted a laugh. "I think Ernie's so funny."

"I think I'm going to vomit. The geriatric crowd shouldn't swivel their hips." Cole backed their vehicle out of the drive and headed up the tree-lined trail to where the ground leveled off above the Beckman brothers' properties.

"How far are we going?" Sam squealed when they hit a bump.

That squeak was so much better than the heavy silence on the ride from town. And if her question was about their relationship, it held a whole lot of meaning, and he only had a partial answer. He wanted Sam to stay in Tennessee, but was he ready to commit to a serious relationship? Was it too soon? Being with Sam was easy. He didn't have to second guess what he said or did. Sam had even renewed his relationship with God. When two people focused on God, there wasn't the time to find faults with everything.

"We can climb as high as you'd like. There's a ridge ahead where the trails widen." He pointed to the north. Ted had taken him out on these trails last summer. He and Ted had traveled all over the property. Jillie Lynn wouldn't ride in the UTV because it messed up her hair. Sam hadn't mentioned her hairstyle once.

When he reached the plateaued path, he parked the UTV. Grabbing flashlights from the console, he handed her one. "Let's go see God's electricity."

When they rounded the hood, he grabbed her free hand. Her skin was soft and warm as if the compassion in her heart flowed freely to every part of her body. She didn't pull away but gripped his hand tighter. He hoped it was because she was beginning to feel something for him and not that she was afraid of falling off the slope. He didn't want this northern beauty to sell Ted's house and return to Wisconsin.

"This sure is a nice piece of property." Cole scanned the rise and fall of all the pines, their shadows decorating the skyline. If he listened carefully, he could hear a slight gurgle from the creek. The cool air enlivened his lungs and gave him a surge of adrenaline. And boldness. "Have you given any more thought to what you'll do with the property?"

Sam faced him. The breeze blew a few strands of hair over her cheek. She attempted to wrangle her hair with her flashlight hand. She didn't unthread their fingers. A good sign.

"I don't know." Their gazes met in the glow of the flashlights. "But seeing everything from up here, Ted's house looks so sad."

Sad was not the mood he was going for. He swallowed past the panic in his throat. "What do you mean?" He recited the verse from Philippians to calm his anxiety. *Do not be anxious about anything.*

"Ted and Nan always decorated for Christmas. Their home was festive and filled with love. It breaks my heart that Ted's home looks so lonely in the dark." Sam sniffled. "Maybe I haven't appreciated Ted's gift as much as I should. It came at a rough stretch in my life."

"Hey." If he was to show this girl how much he cared, it was now or never. Depression and doubt killed the euphoria and romance of stargazing. He shoved his flashlight in his back jeans pocket and grasped her light. "May I?" Setting it on the ground, he rose and stepped close to this woman who stormed into his world and captured his hopes and his heart. He slipped his arms around her waist and drew her into his warmth. She snuggled into his chest. The sensation to protect Sam for eternity flooded his being. "We can string lights once the roof and porch are fixed. I happen to know an electrician who works cheap. You can throw him a few bland cookies."

Her lighthearted laughter against his chest made him grin.

"I mean, we still have a tree to use. LEDs on it will put Ernie's house to shame."

Drawing backward, her gaze searched his face.

God, You sure put this woman together right. Your light in her is shining brighter than the universe.

"Thank you, Cole." She held him a little closer.

A shooting star took flight from his heart.

"For cheering me up with your humor and being cool about…well, earlier." Her tone nose-dived.

"You mean when my old toy became a prop for discussing breast prosthetics." He was not letting her bring embarrassment into this hug.

"No seriously." She swayed in his arms. "I guess I'm still anxious about the cancer. I check in with my oncologist, so I feel pressure to get back to Milwaukee. It's familiar, and well, I have to think about interviewing for a teaching contract." She blew out a breath. "And then there's Christmas."

"You're an only child. Wherever you want to be for Christmas, your parents will show up. There's nothing like a Tennessee Christmas. You probably won't have to shovel out your drive." He brushed a hand through her silky hair. "And I bet you could get a few references for teaching jobs either in Whispering Creek or Sperry's Crossing. Lucinda's reference will be glowing." *Come on, Wisconsin Sam. Stay for Christmas and beyond.* The intensity of that wish had his imagination driving their UTV all the way to the Big

Dipper to wish on the stars. "We do have world class hospitals and doctors in Tennessee, too." His brother was at a top facility.

She worried her lip and then beheld him with those beautiful wide eyes. Her hold on his waist loosened. "Would you like me to stay?" Her lips vanished as her mouth pressed thin.

"Yes, I would." His words came out loud and with a bit of an echo off of the ridge. They didn't scare him. No one was demanding anything from him or trying to change who he was or what he liked to do. "I'd like you to be here for Christmas."

Beaming, she hugged him with the ferocity of a spooked mama bear.

For a moment, he found it difficult to breathe. Sam was strong all right, but was her enthusiasm because she liked him the way he liked her? Would she stay and see where their relationship would lead?

"Ernie was right about the benefits of stargazing," she said, her voice muffled. "Good-hearted men are a temptation in the moonlight."

"Then we better find you a good-hearted man."

"Cole!"

He laughed and tilted her chin toward the stars. "I'd like to steal a stargazer's kiss."

"Under the stars, out in the sun. You may kiss me anytime." She beamed brighter than the moon.

A shot of adrenaline almost lifted him off the ground. He kissed her gently and then showed her with his lips what an amazing woman he thought she was, until he gently ended their kiss.

"You know," he said, enjoying the tingle Sam's mouth left on his lips, "I bet we can find some mistletoe in one of these trees. Let's add that to our weekend decorating list."

"That's if the carpenter and roofer hold to their Saturday date." On tiptoe, she sneaked another kiss.

"Oh, they'll make it. I just wished for it under the stars, and I've got prayers and petitions on the way." He broke their embrace briefly and mimicked Ernie's hip wiggle.

Sam's laughter filled the moonlit ridge. In her delightfully frivolous giggle, he heard relaxed tranquility. Being in a relationship with this woman didn't frighten him. Sam accepted whoever he wanted to be, an electrician, songwriter, or handyman. He felt as if he was flying over the evergreen fields, freer and happier than he had been in years. He wanted Sam to soar along with him.

~*~

Later that night, Cole retired to his room at Ted's place, no, Sam's place. His phone buzzed. A text from his manager appeared. Slater sure knew how to kill a guy's night.

Any progress?

Not with a song, but things were progressing nicely with Sam.

19

Sam lounged on Ted's queen bed, her spine against the wicker headboard. How would she fall asleep after everything that happened today? She had enough energy to race down the lane to Ernie's house and lap the ATV trails. She'd text Emma and find out what was going on in her world. Emma could help sort out these feelings for Cole.

Picking up her phone, she typed *Cole kissed me.*

Instantly, her phone buzzed. Sam answered.

"You can't text me about a kiss with your hottie. I want details. Was it any good?"

"Emma! No." Her bestie acted as though they were back in high school.

"I can tell by that raspy squeal that it passed your test." Emma's laughed loosened the tension in Sam's shoulders. Emma always brought fun and energy to any situation. "Is the bedroom door locked with empty pop cans stationed in front?"

"My bedroom door is locked, but I trust Cole." Cole had made her feel safe and comfortable from the first time he grabbed her and sprinted to shelter in the bathroom.

"I was talking about Cole's door." More giggling laughter filtered through the phone. "You haven't had a great kiss in ages."

"How would you know?" Sam sat forward on the bed. Emma's words held a hint of truth. After the surgery, when Karlton kissed her, he looked as if he was analyzing whether to stick around. Her ex made her self-esteem dive bomb. With Cole, he looked at her as if the kiss had given him glitter wings. She was falling for a guy who valued her inside and out. "I dated Karlton for a while. I thought you liked him?"

"Let's just say Karlton is a cup of decaf and Cole sounds like a pumpkin spice latte with caramel sauce and whipped cream. I'm happy for you." Emma's support bolstered Sam's spirits. "Remember, I get dibs on the brother."

Sam shook her head. Wade would need a shield and body armor if Emma bounced into his hospital room. "He's still recovering from surgery. You'll have to be patient." She grinned at her pun.

"That is bad, sister." A microwave dinged in the background. Emma drank chamomile tea at night. Over the years, Sam hadn't seen much evidence of a calming effect. "Well, if he needs a nurse, I am so there." Pure Emma. Concern and a tease in one sentence. "Tennessee sounds like a blast."

"I don't know with everything I've gone through with the house that's it's been a blast, but I do like Cole." And with Wade's accident, Cole might be living near her new home. God did work in mysterious ways. "Though, Em, sometimes I wonder if the relationship with Cole is moving too fast." She'd been on a rollercoaster since the cancer diagnosis, the surgery, the infection and implant removal, the breakup, Ted's death, the inheritance, and now a new boyfriend. Listing her hills and valleys exhausted her. If her relationship with Cole flamed out, she'd need an extended vacation from stress.

"When it's right, you know it. You've been with him twenty-four seven and haven't kicked him to the curb. Plus, he's a Christian, right?" Em would bring that up since she was the only Christian in her family. She knew what it was like to be ignored or dismissed when she talked about God.

Lord, thank You for bringing Emma into my life, Mr. Ted's life, and into a faith community.

"He's getting back on track with his faith. From what I know about his ex-girlfriend, she wasn't into God." Even if Jillie Lynn wasn't a Christian, it still wasn't right to cheat on Cole and leave a paltry note to say good-bye. Sam's blood pressure spiked when she thought about Cole's ex.

"At least Cole has a faith to go back to. We all make mistakes. If he spent any time with Ted, there would have been a mini-sermon about God." Emma slurped some tea. "I miss those." The teacup clinked on its saucer. "How much does Cole know about your cancer?"

"If you only knew." Sam laid flat on the bed. A faint scent of Ted's subtly spiced cologne remained on the comforter. She sure did miss their wise mentor and friend. "We met a boy named Daniel at a local café, and tonight he popped a squeeze on my prosthetic."

"Did I hear you correctly?" Emma's disbelief

lingered.

"Yep. The little boy grabbed it in front of everyone in the coffee shop." Sam cringed reliving Daniel's inquisitive claw. If she had confessed about her prosthetic at the wiener roast, she wouldn't have been so embarrassed, but then, if she had revealed her secret, Cole may have bolted.

"Cole saw? And he was cool with it?" Emma paused. "Wait. Did the kiss come before or after the fake boob outing?"

Adrenaline surged through Sam's body. She beamed at the bland white ceiling. "After."

"Whaaat? You have got to date this guy, or I will."

"I worry it's too soon after his breakup. Maybe it's a rebound thing for him." That thought weighed on Sam's mind. "I don't know if my heart can take any more drama."

"Hey, what did Mr. Ted tell us?" Emma was in counselor mode. "God knows the plans He has for us, and they're good plans. Pray about the relationship."

Tears stung Sam's eyes. "I am praying. A lot." *Present your requests to God.* "I miss you, Em."

"I miss you, too. When will I see you?" Emma sniffled. "Will you be home for Christmas?"

Sam's heart pained. She didn't like leaving Emma alone for Christmas. "I haven't mentioned anything to my parents yet, but I might stay in Tennessee." She hoped to get a kiss from Cole under the mistletoe and continue what they had started. "There's an open invitation for you to join us. I mean it."

"A cabin in the woods with food and cute guys?"

Intrigue heightened Emma's voice. "I might be able to swing some extra days off. My folks won't be celebrating Jesus' birth unless planets collide. Every time I bring up the subject of God, they shut me down."

"You're welcome anytime." Sam smiled at the thought of her friend in Whispering Creek.

"What was that? I didn't hit record." Emma laughed and then cleared her throat. "No seriously, I'm praying for you. You beat cancer and made it through a bad surgery. You can handle some home repairs and kissing a cute guy." The sound of Emma's teacup echoed over the phone. "Remember, you will always be beautiful to me. And as Mr. Ted would say, God doesn't make any junk. Cancer can't beat God."

Tears flowed down Sam's cheeks. She sat and pulled Ted's Bible into her lap. "Thanks, Em. Everything's been different since the cancer, and you know me so well. Thanks for listening and helping me process my life." She wiped the wetness from her face. "You're the best."

"I know. Now don't make me cry. Go to bed and dream about country boys. I'm praying for you." Emma ended the call. Heart emoji's appeared in Sam's messages with the command, *text me with news.*

Anytime Sam talked with Emma, she felt as if she could win a prestigious marathon. God was Sam's foundation, but Emma was the wind at Sam's back. Lately, Cole had been an encourager as well.

Sam opened Ted's Bible, and the sweet picture of Cole and Ted playing guitar stared back at her. Her heart did a fast twirl. She was falling in love with Cole. "God, I don't know what journey You have me on, but I'm going to trust Your wisdom. You'll give me the strength to handle whatever comes my way. But that guarding my heart and mind verse, well, if Cole gets in his truck and drives away, I'll need Your best security force."

20

Cole exited out of his brother's presentation and glanced at his phone resting on Ted's kitchen table. Quarter to ten in the morning. Where was Sam? Had he freaked her out last night by kissing her? Was she having regrets? Was she practicing her "thanks for everything, but I can take it from here" speech? His truck would be ready this afternoon. He didn't need to stay in the area after tomorrow's pitch. But what did he have to go back to in Nashville? Songwriting wasn't his passion. It had been Jillie Lynn's dream. Wade and Dad were growing the business without him. If it hadn't been for Wade's accident, he'd be odd-man-out as usual.

He traipsed to the kitchen and refilled his mug. He took a swig and glanced at the light fixture in the ceiling, the one Sam needed LEDs for when they met. He grinned as he remembered their adventurous five days. If Sam was having second thoughts, at least he'd have unforgettable memories. Nothing about Sam was boring.

Leaning against the kitchen counter, he tamped down the "less than" taunt that had been playing on a loop since JL left. He relaxed his jaw and closed his eyes.

Lord, I know we haven't talked a lot the past few years. That's on me. I don't know what's next in my life. I'm anxious. Worried about losing Sam to Wisconsin. Losing Wade's bid. Help me, Lord. Starting over is hard. I'm cliff diving here. Please, God.

"Hey, I smell a bold Colombian blend." Sam's ponytail splayed from the back of a Donoven and Son promotional cap. She wore it better than a model. "I'm way overdue for caffeine."

"Coming right up." Sam sounded happy, not apprehensive. He grinned as forty pounds slid from his shoulders. *Thanks, God.* He filled a mug and met her at the table.

She accepted her cup of coffee. "Every time I tried to get ready my phone rang. The front window is being replaced tomorrow. While you're pitching, I'll be supervising. Apparently, the glass is an odd size, but they have it in Jackson."

"Great." By Saturday night, her house would be good as new. If he didn't get the bid for Sperry's Crossing, what excuse would he use to stay in Whispering Creek? Once the window was secure, she wouldn't need a bodyguard. Here he was again, flapping like a broken-stringed kite in the wind. "How about some eggs?" He popped from his seat. Cooking would give him a passing grade. "I do a mean over easy."

"Works for me. A little salt and pepper is fine. Save the hot sauce for yourself." She slouched in her chair and flashed him a smile that would sizzle egg whites. "We'll have to celebrate Saturday night after we decorate."

Celebrate the past, the future, or both? "I'm sure we can find a nice restaurant in these parts." He placed a frying pan on the stove and sprayed it with cooking oil.

"I'd like that. But you know what I'd like more." She untied the wheat bread. "After we light up this place to rival Ernie's…"

He cast a glance her direction and almost cracked his egg on the counter instead of the edge of the pan. Her quirked brow and pursed lips were vintage breakfast flirting.

"I'd like to do some more stargazing." Sam plopped a piece of bread in her mouth and winked.

His cheeks heated faster than the frying pan. He hadn't scared Sam off. In fact, his boots were growing roots right through the tile. Egg in each hand, he swiveled his hips. "Is that what they call it, young lady?" He mimicked Ernie's rebuke in a baritone drawl.

Sam laughed and pointed a sassy finger at him. "For the record, you do that way better than Ernie."

21

Sam signaled and turned off the highway onto the exit ramp for Sperry's Crossing. She had run out of questions for the mock interview she had given Cole, and he needed a break from his computer screen. Scoping out the site of the industrial park would benefit Cole while she had the chance to see more of Tennessee and the surrounding area on the way to Whispering Creek. She prayed Cole would shine and win the bid for Donoven Electric.

In the passenger seat, Cole's lips moved ever so slightly as he stared out the windshield of her SUV. The faint scent of his cedar-based cologne had a hint of something fresh...blueberry? Whatever it was, she'd never grow tired of that aroma.

"Practicing the pitch again?" She glanced at her handsome passenger. He turned his backward baseball cap and sunglasses attitude her direction and whip-started her heart.

Cole scrubbed a hand over his face. "You know what they say, practice makes perfect."

"I tell my students that practice makes permanent. We can't be perfect all the time." She grinned. "It takes the pressure off." And she knew from Cole's family history that the pressure was on big time.

"That makes me feel better. I wish I had a teacher like you." He directed her to take a left at the light. "I'm never going to be as polished as Wade."

Her stomach cringed. Being an only child, she never had to compete for her parents' attention or worry about sibling rivalry. She couldn't imagine navigating that emotional minefield. She slowed the car due to a school zone. "You're talking to guys in the trades, right?"

"I'm guessing a few investors will be there."

"And I bet they're not experts on your..." She flapped her hand trying to pull the right word forward. She failed. "Electrical stuff."

"Now, that's polished." Cole laughed.

"Be yourself." Cole had charmed everyone they had met. Even Ernie. "If you hadn't stepped up, Wade wouldn't even be in the running. I mean, your brother has a long recovery ahead of him. He won't be driving for a while, especially out to Sperry's Crossing. These men and women are meeting you. If they're like me, they will be gazing at you like a star." She tamped down the warmth creeping into her cheeks and glimpsed at her passenger.

Cole leaned over the console. What was he doing? His lips found her cheekbone and planted a soft, oh, so flustering, kiss on her skin.

"Cole!" she squealed his name. "I'm driving."

"You're the one who said practice makes permanent." The rasp in his voice almost had her pulling to the side of the road. Good thing there was a red light ahead. Her insides were joyous enough to do an Ernie hip wiggle in the intersection.

He kissed her cheek a second time and shifted in his seat. "I need to bottle the confidence you have in me and keep it in my suitcoat pocket."

"There's lots more where that came from." She hit the gas pedal and told herself to focus on the road and not the distracting man beside her. Emma had asked if Cole had kissed her before or after the revelation that she only had one breast. The kissing last night happened after, and the kissing continued. If it stopped…? "How much farther?"

Hiding his mouth with his hand, Cole said, "The development is a few miles past this shopping center." Humor riddled his answer.

"I'm trying to be serious here." She couldn't help but smile.

"Yes, ma'am. Me, too." He drummed a soft beat on her dash. "Did you notice the large elementary school back there? Sperry's Crossing is growing."

She had noticed. Noticed how Tennessee's trees and road signs were becoming familiar. Noticed the slight drawl in people's speech when they asked if she wanted sweet tea. Noticed the color of the license plates surrounding her, without the picture of a farmhouse and cheese. And how one songwriting electrician made this state feel more and more like her home. Nashville wasn't too far away, but Sperry's Crossing was whole lot closer. Closer for stargazing.

~*~

An hour later, Cole opened the diner door for Sam. The local barbecue place wasn't far from the industrial park. The tangy, sweet-smelling air had him prepped to inhale a late lunch.

Nothing about the site surprised him after all the perusing he'd done of online maps and the engineer's blueprints. Construction equipment had cleared most of the pines from the parcel of land leaving the conservation area abutting the site untouched. A double-wide trailer was parked near a gravel road, ready to do business with contractors. He hoped Donoven and Son Electric was one of the companies selected.

A waitress showed him and Sam to a booth and handed them menus. The place was crowded, which was a testament to their five-star rating.

"My mouth won't start burning if I order the barbecue, will it?" Her grimace was cute and kissable.

"Nah. You might find it on the sweet side. I put molasses in my recipe." He would have to help Sam up the heat factor in her food. "Would you like some fried okra?"

She stared at him. "Okra? I don't think I've ever eaten that. Don't they have steak fries or fried cheese curds?" Her nose wrinkled as she scanned the menu.

"Try the okra. If you don't like it, you can smother it in ranch dressing." His stomach agreed with a grumble.

After ordering the house barbecue on a bun and fried okra, he reached over and grasped Sam's hand. "What did you think of the industrial park site?"

"It's big." She leaned closer as if they were having a private conversation. "I was picturing a strip mall in my head. Not a small concrete town."

He stroked the back of her hand with his thumb. An upward caress. *Please.* A downward touch. *Stay.*

"Wade is ambitious. There's a lot of wiring to be done. We'll need to hire some help." They wouldn't need to hire as many workers if he came back full-time and stayed in the area near Sam. Wade had been generous with staffing hours. Cole's apartment lease was almost up and with the demand for housing in Nashville, his landlord would shove him out the door and raise the rent.

Was working with his family what he wanted long term? The steady income would be nice. He and Jillie Lynn had some success at songwriting, but not enough to support a family. Songwriters in the country music capital multiplied like sugar ants on honey. *Do not be anxious.*

"Cole?" Sam's hazel eyes searched his face.

"Sorry. I was thinking about the pitch tomorrow. The industrial park looks bigger in person. I was envisioning the buildings on the cleared patch of land." *And the next steps in my life. With you at my side.* He sat straighter ready to engage. He swiped his thumb again on her soft skin. *Please. Stay.*

An older gentleman, in the booth behind Sam, lumbered over to their table, and hovered.

"Are you involved with the construction outside of town?"

Sam withdrew her hands into her lap.

Talk about a water balloon to the face. This guy knew how to kill a mood. Cole would have to remember to keep his voice down. He was accustomed to chatting in loud honky-tonks.

"I hope to be." He nodded. "My company bid on the electrical work." Technically the company belonged to Dad and Wade.

The gentleman crossed his arms over his red fleece vest. "I've got a grandson in an apprenticeship at the moment. He'll be looking for employment. Do you have a card so I can steer him your way?"

"Not with me." Cole had been absent for the past couple years. It would feel good to give a kid a break.

"Here's a notepad." Sam was ready with paper and a pen. Her purse rivaled a department store.

Cole wrote his contact information on the paper.

"Are residents pretty happy with the industrial park going in?" He and Sam were on a reconnaissance mission.

"Mostly. It'll bring jobs and lower taxes. That's what the mayor says." The old man collected the paper and folded it to perfection.

"The conservation area is a nice touch." Sam had a way with older people. She brushed her light brown hair behind her ear and gave him her full attention.

"I was surprised they're building so close to the marsh." The local moved aside when the waitress delivered their drinks. He didn't go away. "I thought they'd leave some room for flooding."

Cole hadn't seen any mention of water issues on the engineer's report. Electrical boxes for the adjacent office space were set fairly close to the conservation lands. Maybe this man's meddling could be helpful. "Does the area flood often?"

Blowing out a pensive breath, the man said, "About every three years. Some time ago they did a study but couldn't find a reason." He shrugged, bunching his Christmas-colored vest. "There was talk of an underground spring nearby."

"That's good to know. I appreciate the information." Cole nodded to the folded paper in the man's hand. "Have your grandson contact me in a week or so. I should know more about my staffing." Cole would be a hero or a zero.

"Will do. Thank you." The man returned to his wife in the neighboring booth.

He reached to rejoin his and Sam's hands and their food arrived. A guy couldn't catch a break in Sperry's Crossing. The aroma of slow-roasted meat, cayenne pepper, and tomato sauce eased his frustration.

"I'll pray." He bowed his head and was interrupted by his phone. What now? His dad's name rolled across the screen. "You go ahead. It's my dad. I should probably grab this in case it's bad news."

Sam bowed her head.

"Hey dad. How's Wade?" His brother could be a pain, but he didn't want to lose him.

"Good as can be expected. I'm here at the hospital. Stopped in before going to work."

And Wade pushed you to call to check on the prodigal brother.

"You'll never guess where Sam and I are." At the

mention of her name, Sam bit into her barbecue. Her eyes widened in a look of ecstasy. Five-star food wasn't a lie. He winked. "We're in Sperry's Crossing."

"Isn't the pitch tomorrow?" His dad sounded concerned. Cole pictured Wade banging his head against his hospital pillow.

"Yeah, it is. We wanted to visit the site. Be as prepared as possible." *I've got this, Dad.*

Sam stared at him as she lazily pierced a piece of fried okra with her fork. Her nose crinkled as she smelled the batter.

"Right." His dad cleared his throat. "Might as well. I uh…I'm praying for God's will."

You. His dad couldn't even say, I'm praying for you. Not in front of Wade.

"Thanks, Dad." Cole swallowed past the ache in his throat. "Tell Wade that I'm praying for his recovery. I'll let you know how the pitch goes."

In the background, before he ended the call, he heard his brother's gratefulness. "Don't blow it."

He flagged the waitress. "I think we'll need some ranch dressing."

22

Sam put on jeans, a shirt with long sleeves, and hiking boots the next morning. She outlined her mouth with vanilla-scented lip gloss and prepared to send Cole off with a kiss and confidence. She hoped his family appreciated the burden they had placed on him. If he didn't get the contract, the tension with his brother would skyrocket. If they accepted Cole's bid, he'd be scrambling to staff the project with Wade expecting to call the shots from a hospital bed.

A call came through on her phone. Mom must be calling before her shift at the hospital because it was 6:04 AM. in Milwaukee. Sam answered with a cheerful hello.

"Hey, honey. It's the big day."

Mom remembered. "Cole's heading off soon. I'm praying the pitch goes great."

"Pitch?" Confusion muddled her mom's voice. "Isn't your front window going in today? The house will be secure now."

Translation—and after the roofers leave on Saturday, you'll be able to come home. Sam avoided mentioning her personal security guard.

"Yeah, I'll feel safer. I didn't expect to have home repairs." Who was she kidding? She never expected to inherit a house.

"Let me know what your plans are, and I'll take some personal days before Christmas. We can go shopping and grab lunch."

Should she drop a hint that she may not be home for Christmas? What was Ted's wisdom? Plant a seed of foreshadowing so roots have time to grow.

Sam checked the time on the digital clock on the nightstand. She didn't want to miss Cole. The coffeepot had wafted its aroma into her bedroom, and she had heard the toaster pop.

"I'm not sure of my plans yet, Mom. I haven't sorted any of Ted's belongings." Or sorted out my life.

"We can help." Pep talk Mom was wide awake. "Remember, the oncologist said to avoid stress. This has been a lot for you to handle."

Not with Cole being here to save her life, chainsaw trees, and set off fireworks on her lips. He had been comforting and accepting of her lopsided chest. He even kissed her after the awkward revelation.

"I'm taking it one day at a time." The truth in that statement scared her. House repairs were tangible. Her relationship with Cole was a blossoming dream, and she didn't want to be living several states away. "Can I call you later, Mom? I know you like to beat traffic, and I need to get ready for the workmen."

"Sure. I love you and want the best for you."

"I know. I love you, too." Having amazing parents added more turbulence to her decision to remain in Tennessee. The longer she stayed in Whispering Creek, the more she didn't want to leave.

She rushed into the kitchen and her heart somersaulted at the sight of her houseguest in a navy suit and caramel-colored wingtips as he was bent over the sink eating toast.

"Good morning." She played nonchalant while an imaginary trapeze artist did flips in her belly. "I came for the send-off."

"Thanks." He put his toast on a napkin and rubbed crumbs from his fingers. "I decided against eggs and hot sauce this morning. My brain is running on a treadmill and my stomach is riding a bull."

"It's a big day, but I have no doubt that you'll do great. You have a way of making people like you." *Including me.* She snuggled her arms under his suitcoat and wrapped them around his waist. He smelled good. Like a warm campfire and a promise of a future.

He smiled as if his whirlwind of emotions had calmed. He kissed her lips and lingered close to her mouth. "Can I get more encouragement afterwards?" He pulled away and rested his forehead against hers. "Will you pray for me? My anxiety level deserves an A plus."

"I'll do you one better. I'll pray with you." She clasped his hand and bowed her head.

"Lord, please be with Cole. Give him strength and help him to remember all that he has studied. Bless his presentation. In Jesus' name. Amen."

"Amen." He hugged her anew. "I'm going to miss you, but I'd better get going. I don't want to get a tardy slip."

She shook her head and gave him a solid kiss on

his lips. Lips that were becoming way too familiar.

Cole gathered his backpack and computer case from his bedroom.

Had anyone from the Donoven family texted to encourage Cole? If Cole hadn't agreed to do the presentation to the investors, the Donoven family would be paddling another creek.

After another too-brief kiss, Cole headed out the door toward his restored truck. Even though it had been gone for a few days, it didn't look out of place.

She strolled onto the porch to wave good-bye.

The truck sputtered, sending the stench of gasoline into the cool morning air. Staccato clicks came from the engine, but it never roared to life. Cole tried to start the engine again but the clicking prevailed. Cole's head rested on the steering wheel.

"Lord, this wasn't in my prayer." Sam raced into her room and grabbed her purse and keys. Her Donoven and Son promotional cap rested on the nightstand. She took that too and sprinted out the front door, stopping briefly to lock it.

Cole halted on the porch steps, hunched under the weight of his belongings.

Flailing a hand for him to retreat, she said, "I'll drive you. I know the way."

"But you have your window being replaced." Cole's big heart was on display.

"It's an eight to noon window." She grinned at her pun and breezed by him. "Come on. We'll stop by Ernie's and Gretta's, and I'll drop off the house key. What are neighbors for?"

Cole headed toward her SUV and thumped the bed of his truck.

"Ernie will love this," she said with a thumbs up to Cole. "He'll think he hit the jackpot. He'll have all morning to snoop inside my house."

~*~

Sam cruised into the industrial site and parked a short distance from the double-wide trailer. Cars with expensive emblems and sleek styles were parked in the gravel lot. Those fancy rides weren't owned by tradesmen. The red truck with the full-size cab most likely belonged to the construction manager.

She faced Cole and winked. "You've got this. Remember, practice makes—"

"Permanent." He kissed her and left the lingering taste of cinnamon on her lips. "Drive by in forty-five minutes and check for a lonely guy in a blue suit."

"Sounds like a plan, but I bet they keep you longer." Smiling, she glanced in the rear seat at the Donoven and Son cap. "I've got some errands to run in town. I'll be praying for you."

Cole hopped out of her car and grabbed his computer bag and backpack. He pointed to the blue sky. "I need a little less anxiety this time, Lord." He grinned as if this was an ordinary occurrence to be pitching for hundreds of thousands of dollars of work. The way he strutted toward the trailer, he could have owned his own company. He was one amazing guy.

She shook her head to stop thinking about his kiss.

Circling her SUV back toward Sperry's Crossing proper, she made a mental list of supplies to buy, and she had a post office to find.

23

As Cole entered the double wide, voices carried from the rear of the trailer. He announced his presence and strode over the upscale laminate flooring toward the sounds. He wiped his free hand on his suit jacket and sent another quick prayer to God. In the back of the office, a large bedroom had been converted into a conference room. No sleeping on the job for this site manager.

A forty-ish man wearing jeans and a blazer met Cole in the doorway.

"Good morning, Mr. Donoven. We were going over your bid, so everyone is on the same page." He held out his hand. "Glen Dawson." Cole gave Glen's hand a firm shake. "I'm the guy the buck stops with. Come in and have a seat, Wade."

Cole's skin tingled. He wasn't Wade, nor could he fill those large loafers. He glanced around the table and owned who he was. He may be Wade's younger brother, but when he was with the company, he was the most requested electrician for service calls, and no one received more plates of thank you cookies.

"I'm Cole Donoven." He acknowledged two men in three-piece suits. One wore a Stetson and a bolo tie. A woman in a blouse and black jeans stood and shook his hand. The brunette reminded Cole of Sam—friendly and prepared for anything. Cole handed everyone a business card. Yesterday, after the diner, Sam insisted they go to a print shop and design a card that he could take with him to the pitch. "My brother was in an auto accident over the weekend. He's fine but has a few broken bones. I'm prepared to answer any of your questions." Cole glanced around the room. "I'm not sure a hospital bed would fit in here."

Muted laughter.

"Will Wade be involved in the oversight of this project?" Mr. non-bolo tie hadn't cracked a smile at Cole's joke or during their introduction. His face was set and his mouth turned down as if he'd just tasted a lemon.

"Wade and I have worked together in the family business for years." Cole emphasized their blood relation. And he hadn't lied. He and Wade had worked well together as long as they stayed out of each other's way. "My brother will be intricately involved."

Mr. Uptight nodded and studied his paperwork.

Cole sat and fired up his computer. He had brought paper copies of Wade's proposal, but everyone stared intently at their devices.

Glen projected the project onto the screen.

Here went nothing, or everything. For the first time since slapping on his electrical hat and returning to help the business, Cole was oddly at ease. The pitch flowed from Cole's mouth, not as an expert, or a Wade wannabe, but as a guy who loved working with his hands and enjoyed showing up at work every day and solving people's problems. He silently thanked the Lord for His peace.

After they had gone over staffing, timing, and budgets, Glen clasped his hands with a commanding clap.

"You've given us a thorough read through of the bid." Glen cast a glance at his associates. "Are there any questions for Cole?"

Thorough? Was Cole a high schooler giving a class report? Glen's choice of wording didn't bolster one's confidence. Energy drained from Cole's body onto the scuffed laminate below.

"I have a question." The put-together woman removed her readers and leaned over the paperwork scattered on the table.

Was this a gotcha question? An attempt to separate the top bidders from the pack?

"All the bids we received were based on the engineering company's excavation reports and designs. Do you foresee any cost overruns?" She tapped her eyeglasses on a copy of the blueprints. "I'm concerned about additional revenue being needed."

Stall. "That's a good question." Should he mention the flooding from the conservation area and deviate from Wade's script? What if meeting the eavesdropper at the diner was a divine appointment?

He cleared his throat. His windpipe seemed to be expanding. "It may be nothing, but I talked to a resident in town. The conservation area that abuts the southeast office space floods every three to five years." The suits shuffled through reports. "If the pattern holds, I'd consider shifting some of the electrical feeds a few feet. It's a minimal cost adjustment at the start. If not done, it would be a cost overrun later and may cause power outages."

Glen placed an aerial view of the property on the screen.

Cole discreetly dried his hand on his pant leg and reached for the laser pointer. "May I show you my concerns?"

The woman crossed her arms over her blouse. "Please do, Mr. Donoven."

Hovering the laser's red dot over the wetlands, Cole prayed his presentation wasn't going up in scarlet flames.

24

Sam reclined in the driver's seat and basked in the warmth from the sunroof. An hour had passed since she'd dropped off Cole at the trailer. She hoped the extra wait meant that his presentation was going well. If Cole secured the project for Donoven Electric, he'd be working in the area. Sperry's Crossing was a lot closer to Whispering Creek than Nashville. If what she was feeling was the beginning of something special, it would be nice to have Cole a short drive away.

She scanned the clear-cut land. Soon companies would build their office and manufacturing space on this open area. Traffic would commute in and out of the park. The makeover of God's earth reminded her of her own recent history. Her life had been on track with a classroom full of students, a boyfriend, and good health, until a lump in her breast changed everything. Parts of her future plans had been cleared away, and she was rebuilding her life day by day. Cancer taught her that every morning was a gift from God. In the oncology department, she had come face to face with patients—some so young, others much older—who had limited tomorrows. Closing her eyes, she willed herself not to cry. Her cancer was gone. Whether she reconstructed her breast or lived with a prosthetic, she would thank the Lord she was alive and parked outside of a trailer in Tennessee.

A bulldozer moved debris in the distance. Rebuilding a life took time. She had time to sort Ted's house and consider a move south. And she had time not to rush.

Cole exited the doublewide and hurried down the stairs. The bounce in his wingtips suggested he nailed the presentation. A surge of excitement had her sitting straighter and quickly checking her face in the visor's mirror. Cole hopped into the SUV's passenger seat and planted a kiss on her cheek. His kisses were fast becoming her favorite greeting.

"You were in there a long time. I hope that means it went well." Otherwise, she would be setting her GPS to Nashville to visit him.

"Let's just say I presented Wade's bid like a sundae and when they asked about cost overruns…" He set his mesmerizing brown eyes upon her. "I added a cherry by mentioning the flooding. I'll know if I cinched the deal on Monday."

Sam prayed the investors appreciated the added reconnaissance because she was fairly certain that Wade wouldn't appreciate his brother's improvisation. Fortunately, Cole would be sticking around for the weekend. Her goal was to make the most of those tomorrows.

~*~

Sam bested the speed limit by five miles per hour

trying to get home from Sperry's Crossing before her window workmen arrived. She turned right after crossing the bridge onto her property. A large blue van, Ernie's station wagon, and Cole's truck were sitting in her driveway. She parked by the shed and jogged up the porch steps.

Cole followed with his backpack and computer bag weighing him down.

Ernie stood with his hands on his hips supervising her window replacement. Gone was the white sheet blocking her view. She could see into the living room through pristine glass. Day one of her repairs was almost finished.

Ernie pointed at the workmen from his station by the front door. "They came pretty soon after you left. Good thing I was around." He dipped his unshaven chin. "They're almost done." If Ernie had an extra hand, he'd probably be patting himself on the back.

"Thank you so much. Cole had an important meeting to get to."

At the mention of his name, Cole turned and winked at her. He was in a deep conversation with a workman about window seals.

Before she gave it too much thought, she gave Ernie a side-arm hug. He stilled like a wooden post. "I'm glad you were here." And she was. Ernie had softened since their first run in. She was pretty sure that was the Gretta factor.

The second workman came through the front door. "We're finishing up. I'll fill out the paperwork for you to sign."

"Wonderful." She stepped aside and let the repairman pass. She unfastened her purse and gathered money for tipping the crew.

Ernie let out a guttural cough that rivaled the clicking of Cole's engine. "We had to move some bookcases that were by the window. I noticed a photo of my parents and my brother and I when we were kids." Ernie's mouth gaped. "I wasn't snooping."

"Of course not." Sam glimpsed crusty ol' Ernie in a new light. Maybe it was because of Gretta's kindness or how Ernie helped out in a pinch, or maybe it was because this was the first time that she saw the sadness in Ernie's eyes over Ted being gone. She and Ernie both loved Ted, though she hadn't shared a family with her beloved mentor and friend. "I would love for you to have the picture."

Ernie nodded. "I appreciate it."

"And you know, neighbor, I haven't started sorting any of Ted's belongings. If you and Gretta have some time to spare, I could use a hand or two. I don't want to throw out any treasures." Sam restrained a giddy smile and gestured for Ernie to go inside her home. "If it's not too much trouble or time to help?"

"Trouble, nah." Ernie had an extra jig in his step as he trudged toward the bookcases. "That's what neighbors are for."

One of the repairmen came inside carrying a clipboard and paperwork. "Ma'am, I need your signature. The window is as good as new."

She withheld a contented laugh. For the first time in a while, so was she.

25

Could he have planned a crazier week? Not if he had tried. Cole placed his truck's key fob in the console's cupholder and pushed the start button. The engine turned over without a click or complaint. Why hadn't his truck worked this morning?

He glanced at the ceiling. "Lord, I don't know what You're trying to teach me, but thanks for providing a backup plan. I would have been in trouble if Sam wasn't here to drive me to Sperry's Crossing." He wasn't sure how many driving services they had around Whispering Creek. Ernie had an extra car, but his grip on its bumper was airtight. With another scenario, Cole wouldn't have received a kiss for encouragement.

How would he ever thank Sam for all her support this week? Sure, he had helped with storm clean up and provided security while her window was awaiting repair, but she drove him to the hospital, prayed with his parents, and gave him the confidence that he needed to ace the pitch. He never imagined meeting a woman at Ted's house that would have him surfing on the wind.

His head was in a fog after the presentation, and he still needed to write a song and send it to Slater.

Come Monday, if he received a contract from Glen Dawson, he'd have to coordinate with Wade and set up a satellite shop of Donoven and Son 2.0.

He collapsed against the leather driver's seat. He just wanted to spend time with Sam and convince her to give Tennessee living a try.

His phone buzzed. *Dad*.

"Hey, Dad. Everything went really well." Cole's temples pulsed. He should have texted. "Wade can relax. The investors were impressed with the presentation. We'll hear on Monday if it's a go. Sorry I didn't let you know sooner. Sam and I just got back, and her window repairmen were finishing up."

"Good to hear. Wade can rest easy now." *It was always about Wade.* "I didn't know Sam went with you."

"My truck wouldn't start. Works fine now, though."

"You probably flooded it. Glad Sam was around." *They agreed on one thing.* "Are you coming back to town?"

"I'm staying in Whispering Creek through the weekend. Sam and I are decorating Ted's house for Christmas." Saturday couldn't come too soon.

"Oh. Are you staying with Sam?" The surprise turned to judgment really fast in his father's voice.

Cole's muscles grew taut. The heat in his truck was nothing compared to the fire flowing through his veins. "She had a sheet for a window."

"That's fixed."

"I know." Simple statements. Why couldn't his dad move beyond questions and commands and casting blame?

"Shouldn't meddle, but I like Sam. She's got her head on straight, and she loves the Lord."

Cole couldn't argue with that wisdom.

"I like her, too." A lot. "I'll let you know what I hear on Monday. Give my love to Mom and text me if there are any updates on Wade."

"Will do. Thanks, Son."

Cole took the thanks from his dad and gift wrapped it because he wouldn't get any from his brother. Wade was making him do penance for leaving the company in the first place.

Ernie ambled down the porch steps, something clutched in his hand. He waved to Cole before getting into the station wagon. Cole waved back. Sam had cracked that acorn with her kindness.

Sam sauntered onto the porch. Of course, she'd give their neighbor a wave and a send-off.

Cole went from being as giddy as a teenager to his gut clenching in anxiety. Dad was right. Sam was safe in her home now, and he shouldn't be living with her. He didn't want people to believe there was more going on at night than a sound sleep. Bringing up the subject terrified him. What if Sam believed he was ghosting her after his presentation? What if she thought her prosthetic was a turn off? What if she soured on staying and went back to her family?

Opening the door to his truck, he whispered a prayer. "I'm trying to do right by You, Lord, and honor my parents. That's a commandment, right? Please help me not to scare off the best thing that's happened to me in a long time. I like the road You have me on. Amen."

He jogged the porch steps, wrapped Sam in a hug, and kissed her soundly.

"Wow! I'll remember to tamper with your truck more often." She grinned and kissed him back. Her flowery scent tempted him to keep the rotation going. His conscience threw cold water on his thoughts.

"I talked to my dad."

Sam drew away, but he gripped her hand. "Is that why you were in the truck so long?" Her lighthearted smile faded.

"Yeah. He was happy about the presentation, but—"

"But?" Sam chewed on her lip as if she knew about his dad chasing him from Ted's house.

"He thinks I need to find a new place to stay since you are no longer living with a sheet for a window."

"That's all he said?" Her eyes blinked as she waited for more of his news.

Sam was taking this better than he expected. "Yeah." He clasped both her hands so he would be her only focus. "I'm thinking my dad may be right. Don't tell him I said that, though." He blew out a long breath. A breath that held regrets from his past relationship. "I'm not proud of some of the things that happened with my ex. I don't want to make the same mistakes in our relationship."

"What does that mean?" Sam nibbled on her bottom lip some more. Her carefree spirit had tumbled to concern, and now it was freefalling. Maybe he shouldn't have mentioned his dad's advice. Ever since he had mentioned his dad, she seemed distracted.

He led her into the house and into the living room. "It means, we find whatever Ted has for Christmas decorations and then drive into Whispering Creek to supplement what we don't have. On Saturday, this place will be the happiest home in Tennessee. Air traffic control might be calling us to dim the lights."

"After Saturday, this place will be back to normal. Everything will be fixed." Sam leaned against the back of the couch and let go of his hand. "Tomorrow, I have an appointment with Chester. He wants to wrap up details on Ted's estate."

Cole rubbed his chin. He wished he could influence the lawyer to counsel Sam to stay in Ted's house. "I'll look for a motel and scout out apartments in the area while you're at the attorney's office." He wanted Sam to know he was serious about their relationship, but she had to want to stay. He had learned that hard truth with Jillie Lynn. "And I do have a song to write."

"That's right." Sam rocked forward and stood. "I almost forgot you were a songwriter with all the electricity talk going on."

"Maybe I should write a song about electricity."

She winked the most beautifully sassy expression. "Or stargazing?" She laughed and tugged him toward the kitchen. "Let's grab some tea and then see if we can find a Bethlehem manger scene or a few plastic poinsettias stashed around here."

Man. He lov...liked this woman. She didn't push him to defy his dad or his beliefs. She was secure in her faith and in her abilities. This woman was a kid magnet and related to people, young and old, in her own special way.

The verse on the devotional his mom had sent flashed through his mind. *I can do everything through Christ who gives me strength.* He hoped that meant convincing his new best friend to stay in Whispering Creek.

26

Sam pulled her SUV into the mini mart to fill her tank with gas. Her meeting with Chester had freed her to contemplate the future without a ticking clock placed on her plans. Ted's attorney had received a payment from a life insurance policy that Ted had taken out years ago. The funds had been overlooked until Chester's assistant had investigated an account and a phone number written on an envelope. The disbursement meant Sam didn't have to hightail it north to work part-time at a floral shop. Her boss said they were doing fine without her.

Getting out of her car, she pushed the button for unleaded gasoline on the pump. With one swipe of her credit card, the rush of fuel began along with the odor of ethanol. Because of Ted's generosity and Chester's assistant's sleuthing, Sam could pay off her card balance. *Thank you, Ted. And thank You, Lord.*

Many prayers had been said on her behalf over the past months. Prayers for successful surgeries. Prayers for healing. Prayers for a new teaching contract. God had seen fit to answer some of the requests. Her cancer was gone. Her infection was gone. Her teaching position was still in limbo. Or was it? With Ted's generosity, she had a home, a lump sum of income, new friends, and time to search for a new job. Perhaps when she petitioned God for a classroom in Wisconsin, He had smiled and thought, *wait for it*. God knew the plans He had for her. Maybe her classroom was hundreds of miles south in Tennessee.

The nozzle *thunked* signaling a full tank while simultaneously emphasizing the mention of Tennessee.

"Sam." A woman's voice broke into her daydreams.

Lucinda waved from the front of the mini mart. She rushed over, a plastic bag swinging from her arm.

Replacing the nozzle into the pump, Sam walked around the cement foundation to greet Lucinda.

"I'm so glad I saw you." Lucinda's long dark hair brushed against the fabric of her pea coat. "I wanted to thank you again for the tree. I've had so many compliments on it. Daniel and I ordered some dinosaur ornaments for it online."

Sam smiled at the mention of her tiny dinosaur enthusiast. "I hope the ornaments don't roar." She laughed. "I'm happy you're enjoying the tree. Cole and I are going to decorate the other uprooted one tomorrow."

At the mention of Cole's name, Lucinda switched the bag in her hands. Her shoulders slumped as if the bag contained boulders. "I feel so bad about your cancer and the embarrassment you must have felt at the café."

"Don't feel bad." Sam clutched Lucinda's free hand. "Daniel was being curious and honest. I would've had to tell Cole eventually about losing a breast."

"He didn't know?" Lucinda's stunned exclamation had a man who was pumping gas glance their direction.

Sam didn't need another public announcement about her deformity. Leaning closer and lowering her voice to a whisper, Sam said, "He knows now." She laughed as if sharing a joke with a confidant. "I didn't know how to tell a guy I've known less than a week that one of my girls was missing."

"Seriously?" Lucinda unclasped Sam's hand and rested her hand on Sam's shoulder. Through her raincoat, Sam felt the slight massage of Lucinda's fingers. "You've only known him for a few days?"

"Since the storm last Saturday. It stranded him at my house when the bridge onto Ted's property was blocked." Sam almost grinned. Her response sounded like a light-hearted romance novel or movie.

Lucinda squeezed tighter. "For the record." Her tone became motherly. "I thought you two had been dating for a while. Cole is certainly taken with you."

"Thanks." Sam was certainly taken with Cole. To the moon taken. "We'll see where it goes."

"I'd better get back to work." Lucinda removed her comforting hand. "Daniel talks about you two all of the time. And I mean all of the time. Please come by again soon. Oh." Lucinda's face lit up. "I almost forgot one of the reasons that I rushed over here. Give me your number and I'll text you mine. There may be some teaching positions opening up at the school." Lucinda added Sam as a contact on her phone. A *ding* sounded from Sam's pocket. "Daniel's teacher won't be returning, and another teacher is retiring. I'll get in touch when I know more."

"Great. I'm very interested." Sam waved as Lucinda rushed to her minivan parked near the entrance to the quick market. "We'll stop by soon."

Sam walked around the rear of her SUV near the edge of the gray metal overhang protecting all of the pumps. A beam of light radiated through the clouds casting a shine on whatever it touched.

Laughing to herself, Sam said, "I know you're in control God. I just wish you had numbered the steps I'm supposed to take on a bulletin board."

27

Saturday morning, Cole shoved warm scrambled eggs into his mouth and reviewed his song lyrics. His legs tried to get comfortable under the table in the cramped booth at the motel's restaurant. He was still hyped from the presentation. Yesterday, he had found a few apartments that looked promising near Sperry's Crossing. No matter what transpired with the bid, he had done his best.

The stress of living up to Wade's expectations had certainly amped his prayer life. He prayed for God's will, and he hoped God's will included a business venture near Whispering Creek and that a certain teacher fell in love with Tennessee and with him. One petition was looking good so far. Tonight, after Sam's porch and roof were fixed, they would celebrate the end to this crazy week with decorating her home and enjoying a nice romantic dinner.

Sipping his coffee, he stared at his lyrics and tried to recreate his songwriting muse without Ted, Sam, or the landscape of Whispering Creek.

His phone rang, breaking his concentration, or lack of it.

Dawson Construction flashed on the screen.

Cole's heart jack hammered. He reached for his

phone and rammed his elbow into the edge of the faux wood table. Pain radiated down his arm. He answered the call while rubbing his aching bone.

"Cole Donoven." He conjured a cool and composed voice.

"Cole, it's Glen Dawson. Hope I'm not calling too early." With Glen's chipper greeting, Cole prayed the manager wouldn't dump cold water on his life.

"No. I was already working." True, but on a song. Cole sat straighter and hoped deep breathing would help him process the news better, good or bad.

"I know I said I'd call on Monday, but I thought you could use some extra time to swing into gear with your brother's accident. You won the bid. The board was impressed with the detail of your proposal, and the fact that you talked with residents of the town."

Fisting his hand, Cole shot it toward the ceiling, ignoring the dull throb in his elbow. If he wasn't in a restaurant, he would have shouted a whooping yes!

"That's great news." Cole's insides were all awhirl. Who should he tell first? What did he need to do first? Firsts were multiplying in his brain. "We are looking forward to working with you as well."

"We ask you keep the news under your hat until Monday afternoon. We have companies to notify." Glen had slipped into manager mode. "We don't want anything posted to social media. This is a courtesy call."

"Got it. I'm happy to sit on the news." Maybe that was best for Wade's health too. His brother would work non-stop instead of rest. His family wasn't expecting the news until Monday anyway. "I appreciate your consideration of Wade's accident."

"I'll be in touch early next week. Congratulations."

"Thank you, Glen." *Thank You, Lord.*

Cole collapsed against the overstuffed leather booth. His whole life had been set on a different path. An exciting, exuberant, yet frightening path.

His phone rang again. He jerked to answer it. Had Glen forgotten something? Cole's finger was on the green button before he glanced at the top of the screen. Stephen Slater. Talk about a downer. Fortunately for his manager, Cole had the beginning of some lyrics and a melody.

Cole gave an upbeat greeting to his bulldog manager. He wouldn't be dealing with Slater much longer.

"Whatcha' doin'?" The sultry purr on the line wasn't coming from Slater. His arms tingled from a cool rush of adrenaline as his heart raced. "Jillie Lynn?" Saying her name placed a yoke of dread upon his shoulders. "Why are you calling me on Slater's phone?" Because she was an expert game player. A fraud pretending to be what Sam embodied.

"You blocked me. How was I supposed to get in contact with you to finish our song?" Her full-blown pout mode came through loud and clear.

"Thought you were in Europe." *With the man you dumped me for.* His mind slogged through the mud pit that had been his life with her. She'd dragged him down, and he'd not realized it until now. But not anymore.

"I was, but Trystan and I are done, so I came back to Nashville." Her voice was ethereal as though she was killing time and her betrayal hadn't even happened. "Why don't I come by your apartment, and we can collaborate?"

Being alone with her was poison. His ex could play the wounded girl all she wanted. He had learned his lesson and moved on to a woman with an authentic heart. "Can't." A short answer that held a lot of wisdom. "I'm in Whispering Creek."

"Meet in a public place and get the song done." Slater's brokering sounded through the phone.

An eerie hum settled in Cole's ears and clanged a warning into his brain. Didn't Slater know what he was asking? Slater was picking at the stitches dissolving in Cole's heart. He blew out a long breath. Stupid songwriting contract. The song commitment was what tied him to Jillie Lynn. If he got it finished, he wouldn't have to see her again or be hounded by his music manager. This could be a clean break, a final good-bye, closure to a big mistake. Closure before he started the work in Sperry's Crossing.

His gut continued to tell him to run fast and never look back. He pinched the bridge of his nose. *God what are You doing here?*

"How will you get to Whispering Creek?" He muttered logistics hoping for an out. "A shared ride can be expensive." The bank of Cole had closed.

She giggled, carefree, but with a dagger tip at the end. "I have a new vehicle."

He wanted to be done with this impostor of a

girlfriend. He was ready to start fresh, having repented of his past. If he met her, where could he go that was safe? With witnesses? A place he could go where the devil wouldn't deceive him about his relationship with this woman and resurrect the fool he had been. Stifling a rude comment, he focused on his future with Sam.

"There's a coffee shop in Whispering Creek called A Brew 4 You. Meet me there at 11:00 AM." He ended the call before she could protest.

Slumping in the booth, he prayed this was truly the end. He had given up his friends, family, and a comfortable lifestyle to be with a woman who used him. He was working on forgiveness. Of her, of himself, of all the mistakes he had made. Forgiveness was a long process.

He stared at the lyrics he had written in his notebook.

You left me at a crossroads, with two lanes I didn't feel like taking,

But sometimes when you head in the wrong direction, you wind up where you're supposed to be.

So, walk, walk, walk away in that form fitting dress,

I'll do my best to clean up the mess,

When you're gone, gone, gone,

You're gone for good,

Babe, let's be certain that's understood.

Someone once told me that good-hearted men are a temptation in the moonlight,

That holds true, so true, 'cause I've already found someone new.

He closed the notebook and ate his last bite of egg.

The coagulated yellow mass had grown cold and tasteless. If that wasn't a metaphor for his memories of Jillie Lynn...*I am so done with Jillie Lynn, Lord. Help me stay strong.*

He prayed Daniel would be running around the café roaring with his T-Rex. Truth be told, he wouldn't shed a tear if a real T-Rex consumed Jillie Lynn when she entered the coffee shop.

~*~

Cole lugged his guitar through the door of the coffee shop. The cinnamon scent with a hint of pine thrown in for holiday cheer couldn't ease the feeling that with each step he would fall into a dark abyss. The Christmas tree sparkling in the corner reminded him of Sam. How he missed her. She was busy with her roofers and carpenter today. He prayed coming clean about this rendezvous wouldn't harm their relationship. He'd spill about the meeting mid-entrée tonight.

He rolled his shoulders as he surveyed the room for the perfect table. A table in full view of the diners. He needed a double helping of strength not to race out of the door. Hadn't Joseph fled Potiphar's wife, leaving his clothes behind? Mankind hadn't changed much.

Lucinda approached with her hostess smile. "Are you going to serenade the lunch rush?"

"Maybe later." He set his guitar case on the floor.

"Is Sam coming?" Lucinda glanced toward the entrance.

His stomach hollowed. Confession time. "I wish. I'm actually meeting my ex."

"Oh." Lucinda's short answer held a whole lot of attitude.

"My songwriting manager wants one last song." He held up a hand in surrender. "Last song. Last time. And this is the only place that I have back up. I don't want to be alone with her." He argued his case with a forlorn grimace.

"Will you tell Sam about this meeting?" Lucinda's interrogation had begun.

"Over a romantic dinner."

"Roses would help." Lucinda pointed to an open table. "Take table nine. I'll send Daniel over when she gets here."

"Thanks. I owe you one."

She shot him an understanding look. "Unfortunately, I know about bad relationships."

Unfortunately, he did too. Settling into a chair against the far wall of the restaurant, he set his keys and phone on the table. Opening his guitar case, he placed a pen, a copy of the lyrics, and his latest melody on the tabletop. He grasped the neck of his guitar and cradled it on his thigh.

The jangle of the doorbells jolted his heart. Jillie Lynn's entrance brought a foreboding he needed a machete to slice through. Her heels clacked across the wooden floor. In tight, torn jeans and a black leather top, more than a few older guys turned to follow her path. She slung a studded jean jacket over the chair across from him and wafted the stench of cigarette smoke his direction.

"Hey." She slid into her seat, drenching him with her sickly-sweet perfume and gaslighting him with a smile that had forgotten her betrayal. Bending forward as she adjusted her chair, she flashed him a swell of cleavage. "You should have come into the city. There's nothing to do out here. Well." She giggled and winked.

Her well-rehearsed charms wouldn't work this time. How many men had she used them on since Trystan?

"Except write." He strummed a chord. "I've got the beginning of a song." He indicated the paper on the table before her. She didn't look down.

"You've grown out your hair. I like it." She batted her eyes and pursed her lips as if he were a thousand-dollar bill that she was enticing into her pocket. If she only knew how stale her tricks had become.

Daniel chugged toward the table with the same hand-me-down dinosaur figurine Sam had given him. Lucinda had remained true to her promise. Cole let out a silent thank You to God.

"Co." The boy halted by Cole's side of the table and scrunched his nose at Jillie Lynn. "Where's Sam?" Daniel timidly touched the strings on the guitar.

"Who's Sam?" Jillie Lynn tapped her blue acrylics on the table. "Can he take this kid away?"

"She gives me stickers." Daniel did his hyper dance and ended it with an exaggerated hop in Jillie Lynn's direction.

His ex shifted away from Daniel.

Daniel hovered closer to Cole and plucked another

string. "Dinosaur stickers. In her purse."

What Cole wouldn't give to wrap Sam and Daniel in a grizzly bear hug.

"I'm not carrying a purse." Jillie Lynn ignored the boy and glanced at the song.

Lucinda swept over with two mugs of coffee. *Bless her*.

"Let me know if you need menus," Lucinda said, bug-eyed.

"What we really need is for you to remove your son. If he's yours." Jillie Lynn nodded her blonde extensions in Daniel's direction.

Lucinda stiffened and cast a roaring lioness glance at Cole.

"Relax, JL. Daniel's a friend." So was Lucinda, and he wanted to keep it that way. "I played some Christmas songs here the other night. Daniel helped me strum." He smiled at Lucinda. "We're fine with coffee."

Lucinda gave a curt nod and tended to the next table.

"I have a melody for the lyrics I wrote." The faster they got down to business, the faster Jillie Lynn would leave. He repositioned himself so Daniel could watch his finger placement. He pushed the words to the song closer to Jillie Lynn. "This is what I have so far."

As he began to play, Jillie Lynn's shoe rubbed against his ankle. He moved his foot. Undeterred, her heel stroked higher on his calf.

Jillie Lynn leaned across the table, her tan line rising on high tide above the black leather. "We don't need company," she whispered.

He remembered the simmering gaze beneath her false eyelashes. His former self would have scooped her in his arms and sprinted her out of the café. Now, the predatory gleam sickened his intestines.

Cole bent under the table and snatched her foot, stilling the caress of his leg. He set her high-heeled foot as far from his boot as possible.

Daniel squatted to peruse the new game. "No kicking." He waggled a finger at Jillie Lynn.

The boy made a great wing man.

Jillie Lynn scowled. "Does the kid really need to be here? We have business to finish. Or..." Her perfectly sculpted eyebrows arched. "Some unfinished business to discuss?"

"It's over." The harshness in Cole's retort stunned him.

"We were on a break." Jillie Lynn reached across the table.

He gripped his guitar tighter and left her arm splayed on the tabletop.

"No, you were on a break and cheated on me."

Daniel jumped from his chair and raised his T-Rex high. "No cheating."

"You've got that right, buddy." Cole messed Daniel's hair.

The boy roared.

Leaning back in her chair, Jillie Lynn crossed her arms. "So, the someone new in the song. That's Sam? Your new fling?" Before he could answer, Jillie Lynn snapped her fingers for Lucinda. "Can I get a carafe of hot coffee?"

"Right away." Lucinda's answer was as sweet as JL's perfume.

Roses for Sam. Roses for Lucinda. Roses for the whole restaurant.

"Our song needs a woman's anthem." Jillie Lynn grabbed the pen and wrote on the page. "Your words are like every other ballad at the bottom of the charts." She marked up his lyrics. Better she attack the paper than attack him with her claws.

"It's our last shot, so make it good." He helped Daniel play a few strings on the guitar while Lucinda returned with a pot of coffee and fled.

Jillie Lynn narrowed her eyes. "Take that kid away before I say something unfit for little ears."

Jaw clenched, Cole set his guitar aside and grabbed Daniel's hand. "Come on, buddy. I promise we can play a song later on." *When this woman is out of my life for good.*

Daniel's head hung down, but he grabbed Cole's hand. Cole led him to the front counter. Bending on one knee, he said, "I'll bring Sam next time, and we can hang out. OK?"

"OK." Daniel hugged his dinosaur and waited at the counter.

When Cole returned to the table, Jillie Lynn texted furiously. On his phone.

Panic set in. "Hey, what are you doing?" He tried to sound calm, but his heartbeat thudded in his ears.

The beastly beauty stood and held his phone in the air. "Acting like a brat." She opened the lid to the pot of coffee and dropped his phone in the hot liquid. Once it sank, she closed the lid.

His mouth gaped. He lunged to retrieve his phone. "Ahh." Coffee burned his fingertips. What had he done to deserve this? He flapped his throbbing hand. And who was she texting?

"I'll finish the song and give it to Stephen. Much improved." She smirked her blood-red lips. "Don't call me," she said too loudly for the café space. She strutted away from the table, her bedazzled jean jacket slung over her shoulder. Turning, she feigned shock with a hand to her cheek. "Oh, I forgot. You can't call." A wicked cackle followed her out of the coffee shop.

In the café, clinks and conversation evaporated.

Heat advanced from Cole's neck to his forehead as patrons stared. Jillie Lynn had commanded center stage where she always craved to be.

Lucinda rushed over. "Are you all right? I am so sorry about your phone. I wouldn't have brought a full pot if I'd known she planned to dunk it."

He would have purchased a new phone weeks ago, if that was all it took to banish Jillie Lynn and her memory from his life.

"It's not your fault." He rubbed his chin. "It's better the phone got scalded than my lap. I'm actually relieved your shop is still standing. No broken glass or overturned tables." He half-heartedly grinned at Lucinda. "Can I borrow your phone to call my manager? I'd better warn him that she's in a mood."

"Sure." Lucinda slid her phone from her apron pocket and handed it over.

Slater answered on the first ring. "I guess congratulations are in order."

"You'll get the last song. Jillie Lynn is on her way with my lyrics and music." He sat back down and turned away from the gawkers. "She's promised to finish it."

"The song? I was talking about your engagement?"

Sweat beaded on Cole's lip. "Engagement? What are you talking about?"

"I received a group text announcing that you and JL are getting married."

Cole's gut clenched. "No. That's a lie. We're done."

"I figured." Slater's congratulatory tone sobered. "You don't sound like a giddy groom-to-be."

Blood chilled in Cole's veins. "Who else was on that text?"

"Uh, your mom and a guy named Sam Williams."

Closing his eyes, Cole slumped in his chair and ended the call. This couldn't be happening. He was starring in a nightmare.

A tapping came upon his shoulder.

"No cry, Co."

28

With the carpenter and roofers paid and gone, Sam stood in the driveway and admired her fixed-up house. She embraced her new cute, country home and the promise it held. She pictured Cole the day they had met, leaning against the threshold in his jeans and form fitting black shirt, scaring off Ernie, and whisking her to safety from the storm. Her skin tingled at the vision of Cole. Hurry up decorating and dinner.

Kicking at some pebbles on the asphalt drive, she breathed in the fresh air and pushed up the sleeves of her glittery red sweater. The tree leaning against the shed, which was soon to be a Christmas beacon, gave off a tangy aroma of sap. Peacefulness exuded from the wooded creek and surrounding evergreens. She understood why Ted had chosen this scenic property near family. Why had she been in such a rush to leave? Rent didn't need to be paid. Teaching contracts weren't coming out until March. If Lucinda was correct, an early-elementary position would open up in Whispering Creek. Sperry's Crossing was an option, too. Mild winters were a huge draw. But the biggest draw was a man who accepted her scars and all.

She strode inside after admiring her solid porch and heard her phone ding. Her phone rested on Ted's

Bible in the bedroom. Was Cole finished with his work early? Maybe he wanted to catch lunch and dinner?

Jillie Lynn and I are getting married.

The bedroom felt like it was floating to a thunder-filled sky with her in it. Was this a joke? The message came from Cole's number. She plopped on the bed and re-read the nightmare lettering. Had the past week been a lie? The camaraderie, the confessions, the kissing? Had Cole been two-timing her just as Karlton did? Had he been stealing kisses under the starlight and texting his ex when she wasn't around? Whispering Creek was starting to become her home, and now her memories were a cruel hoax?

Tears welled in her eyes. Cole wasn't getting off the hook with a text. She called his number, but it didn't go through. She'd been left in the dust.

Who was she kidding? Cole played the accepting boyfriend to protect her feelings while he needed her, but who wants a girlfriend with scars and one breast? He had done what Karlton had done, pretended her deformity was no big deal. Well, it was a big deal. A big deal breaker. Stupid cancer. Sure, get another lick in, why don't you? A droplet slid down her cheek and splattered on her jeans darkening the denim. Why did Cole let her believe she was normal? Why did he let her hope that they might someday be setting up a home together?

She wished Ted was here to share his wisdom. Nan, too. *God has someone special for you, Sammy. He's in the business of establishing Christian homes.* She glanced at Ted and Nan's picture on the dresser and sobbed.

With all that had happened the past week, she had never visited Ted and Nan's grave. Maybe even from heaven, they could soothe her heartache.

Her phone rang. Lucinda's name flashed on the screen. She didn't want to talk about a teaching position now. Her future was on a seesaw again. What if Cole had stopped by the café and told Lucinda his news? Sam didn't need any more pity.

She turned off her phone. Her moments of peacefulness had been trashed by a text. Or had they? She didn't have to wait for Cole in this empty house. Grasping Ted's Bible, she retrieved her purse and car keys and decided to pay her respects to her former neighbors. Ernie or Gretta could tell her how to get to the cemetery. No one could hurt her there. Everyone was dead.

As she shut the door to the house, Gretta and Ernie pulled into her driveway. *Great timing, God, but I could have used a minute.* How would she explain her puffy face? She forced a smile and jogged toward Gretta's rolled-down window.

"I made some more cookies for you." Gretta balanced the plate on the windowsill. Her jovial expression fell. "Are you OK, honey?"

"Yeah." Total dodge. "I was thinking about Ted and Nan, and I got emotional." Sam took the gingerbread cookies and balanced them on top of the Bible. "Thank you for the treat." She cleared her throat. "I thought about visiting the cemetery. Is it close by?"

"Oakwood Cemetery. It's on the south side of the county road." Ernie's head bounced around like a toddler with Gretta blocking his view. "Take a left once you get over the bridge."

"Would you like some company?" Gretta sounded like Mom. Concerned, but wary of where the tide of emotion may travel.

Sam sensed another poor-me sob coming on. "Thanks, but I'd rather go alone. I appreciate the treats." She raised the plate and hurried around the front of the station wagon, rushing to her SUV. She waved as Ernie put the wagon in reverse. She should have known Cole was too good to be true. He didn't like Christmas cookies unless they sizzled on his tongue. Her eyes started to throb. This Christmas, baristas and country music cowgirls were on her naughty list.

Teary-eyed, Sam drove to the cemetery. She couldn't miss Oakwood. The name was big and bronzed into a fieldstone wall. She parked at the reception building and received directions to Ted's plot. A few people visited graves in the distance on the other side of the large oval drive. Huge oak trees similar to the ones that had blocked her bridge gave the grounds a restful, neighborhood park atmosphere. Ted and Nan's marker was a dark slate gray and stood out from the lighter gray and limestone markers surrounding their resting place. *Always make assignments easy to read.* A true Ted-ism.

She hugged Ted's Bible to her breast, the one that would collapse with ease. A slight gust danced the leafy shadows of a nearby oak across the engraving of Psalm 46:1 on the headstone. "God is our refuge and strength." Sam could use some of that strength right about now.

"I finally made it to Tennessee, Ted." She licked her lips and tasted salt. "I met your friend, Cole." *Wish I hadn't.* Darn if her eyes didn't flood again. Deep down, she knew her thought wasn't true. "You were so generous in giving me your house, but it's so far away from Milwaukee. I'm trying to figure out if I should stay in Tennessee or go back to the cold."

Was she waiting for an answer? She sat on the mature grass on Nan's side of the gravestone and opened Ted's Bible. The picture of Ted and Cole playing guitar slipped to the ground. Seeing Ted and Cole smiling, slayed her heart. She retrieved the picture and held it above the pages.

"I truly hope you're happy, Cole."

She couldn't understand how Cole could be happy with Jillie Lynn from what she had gleaned about the diva over the past week. Flipping to Psalm 46, Sam began reading.

God is our refuge and strength, an ever-present help in trouble.

The words from one of Ted's favorite verses jingled Christmas bells in her heart. Sam needed refuge. She needed strength. She needed to seek God. And God was in Tennessee as much as He was in Wisconsin.

29

Insides churning, Cole drove out of town. He had to tame his language as he cursed every red light. He prayed Sam was busy with the workmen and that her phone was tucked away inside the house. Only Jillie Lynn could turn one of the best mornings of his life into a catastrophe. His ex would never be content. He saw that now after she attempted to ruin his happiness. Twice.

He pressed the gas pedal, trying not to speed too much. His hands ached from strangling the steering wheel. *Lord, I could use Your help here because anxiety is my middle name.* Traveling over the bridge, he stopped in front of Sam's place. His insides plunged into an abyss. Her SUV was gone, and the work on the roof and porch was completed. If Sam had driven somewhere then she had her phone and she had seen the text.

His fingertips tingled as he tapped the wheel. Where would Sam go? Hopefully, not home to Wisconsin. He slumped in the seat and dragged a hand over his face. Gretta and Ernie might know where she went. If she had left for a while, she would need them to look after things.

He was at the Beckmans' doorstep in less than a

minute, charging up their steps without shutting off his truck. He knocked on the door, relieving some of the tension in his muscles. He would have kept pounding if it wasn't rude.

The door opened.

"Cole?" Gretta balanced on her boot. "It's good to see you." Even Gretta's baby powder and rose perfume couldn't calm his internal engine.

"Do you know where Sam is?" His blurted question wasn't neighborly, but he'd apologize later.

"Yes, yes I do." Gretta's answer was angelic. "We saw her earlier. She asked us where the cemetery was because she wanted to visit Ted's grave."

He slouched against the doorframe. Sam hadn't left the state.

Ernie angled next to his wife. "You two have a fight? It's the first time I've seen you apart."

"Sort of." How did he condense the morning into a sentence? "My ex-girlfriend sent Sam a text that we were back together and then trashed my phone. My ex didn't like lyrics I had written about Sam."

"Oh, my." Gretta's exclamation exuded pure sympathy. "No wonder Sam had been crying."

Ernie scratched his chin. "You showed your ex a song you wrote about Sam? That's like fishing for stupid with two worms."

"Ernest." Gretta's eyes widened at her husband.

"I'll explain later, but for now, where's the cemetery?" Cole backed toward his truck while Ernie gave directions.

Cole rehearsed his apology as he sailed down the

county road. When the cemetery came into view, he entered by the visitor's center. Sam's SUV drove toward him on a lane that looped around the cemetery.

He sped her direction, honked his horn, and swerved to block her car. He burned a little rubber, but it wasn't a blaze.

Sam slammed on her brakes.

Jumping out of his truck, he raced around the tailgate.

"Are you insane!" Sam stormed his way, arms flailing. "This is a cemetery. Not a racetrack." Her eyes were like two flame throwers, but his body was already scorched.

"I know." He reached his hands toward her. "Let me explain."

"You could have called or texted instead of causing a scene." She crossed her arms and stuck out her shapely hip. Even mad she was stunning.

"No, I couldn't." He ran a hand through his hair surprised it wasn't totally gray. "Jillie Lynn trashed my phone in a pot of coffee. After she sent that false text about us getting married." The word married and Jillie Lynn in the same breath made him sick.

Sam's nose wrinkled. "How'd she get your phone?"

Honesty had better be the best life insurance policy. "I met up with her to finish one last song." He emphasized the finality. "When I was busy with Daniel—"

"Wait. Our Daniel? Dinosaur Daniel?" Sam's hands were talking too. "You were at Lucinda's café?"

"I needed back up." From the disgruntled teacher expression aimed at him, he was getting a failing grade. "Witnesses to say nothing happened and to keep Jillie Lynn in line." He glanced toward the blue sky. *Help me, Lord.* "I want to be with you, not her. JL flipped out over lyrics about you and new beginnings and moonlight."

Sam wrapped her arms around her waist. "You and Jillian haven't been broken up long."

"We're not together." He stepped closer. "I should have told you about the meeting, but I didn't want you to get hurt. And you got hurt anyway. I'm sorry." He opened his arms for a hug. "Will you forgive me?" His heartbeat boomed all the way to his toes as he stood there, arms extended, waiting, just waiting for a twitch or a baby step. "I only want to stargaze with you."

A few renegade tears dripped from Sam's eyes and settled on the curve of her smile. "Apology accepted." She sauntered into his embrace.

Holding Sam in his arms, had him soaring above the oak trees. "Hey Nan and Ted," he called out over the gravestones. "I'm crazy about your former neighbor."

Sam laughed against his chest. She pulled away from him ever so slightly. "You know, I'm going to have to look at those song lyrics." From the smile she bestowed, his failing grade had risen to a solid B. Later, during their home decorating, he'd make sure to pass with an A. Plus. Plus. Plus.

~*~

How could a cemetery be so romantic? Sam held onto Cole next to a tall, moss-covered monument, and she wasn't letting go anytime soon. She held on without a thought to prosthetics, loss, or rejection. Her emotions had soared this morning, crashed over a text, and now she was ecstatic. She held in a giggle about static electricity as Cole's body warmed her like a hot bubble bath.

Whether Cole had returned or not, God had plans for her. Good plans. The best plans. The more she remembered all of her blessings, the more living in Whispering Creek appealed to her even if it was a tiny bit scary.

"Hey." Cole's voice rumbled close to her ear. "I got a call this morning from Glen Dawson. About the industrial park."

A burst of energy had her bouncing on tiptoe and almost coming eye-to-eye with Cole. She scanned his face for the answer, but all she saw was her reflection glistening in his hypnotic gaze. "Well?"

"Let's just say I'm going to have to make a decision on the apartments I checked out yesterday." He grasped her hand, backstepped from their embrace, and scrubbed his other hand over his mouth and chin. "I'm still in shock."

"What did your dad say?" She swallowed past a pull in her jaw.

Cole laughed. "He doesn't know. I need to keep the news quiet until Monday." His exuberance tempered. "I should tell both Dad and Wade, together, in person if you're up for another trip to Nashville?"

"Eat your mom's cooking and clean out more closets?" She kissed him on the lips. "When do we leave?"

"My mom!" Cole thumped his forehead. "Can I use your phone? You weren't the only woman to receive Jil—my ex's text. I hope my mom has her phone stashed somewhere out of the way."

"Mine is in my car." She tugged him toward her SUV and handed him her phone.

Cole sniffed the air. "I smell molasses."

Men and their stomachs. "Gretta made us some gingerbread cookies." She offered him the plate. He lifted the green holiday plastic wrap and withdrew a gingerbread man.

"Way to go, Gretta. This one has red hots for eyes and buttons." He took a big bite and devoured his treat using only one hand. "Mm mm."

"I'll stick with raisins." She shook her head and glimpsed the Bible, the edge of the photograph sticking out from its pages. "I've got a question." She showed the guitar picture to Cole as he finished his text. "This was in Ted's Bible."

"I remember that photo." Cole straightened his black jacket as he studied the snapshot. "Ted didn't think he could learn to play guitar, so I showed him a simple song. He told me he would pray for me. At the time, I thought he was referring to my music, but now I know he meant a whole lot more." His voice cracked as he shared about his friendship with Ted. "We should frame this one."

She came alongside him and rubbed his back, the

material smooth on her skin. "Looks like Ted's prayers and petitions worked."

"Boy, did they ever." He bent down and gave her a cinnamon red-hot kiss.

A kiss filled with a whole lot of confidence and a whole lot of zing.

30

On Sunday, Sam and Cole attended Whispering Creek Community Church and then headed to Nashville to deliver the news about the Sperry's Crossing project. While Sam helped Cole's mom prepare dinner, Cole had gone to replace his phone and stop at the hospital. Cole's dad was keeping Wade company.

Sam's phone flashed a call from Emma. Excusing herself, Sam stepped outside into the brisk air to talk to her friend. Her bestie had finally listened to her voicemail.

"You're staying for good?" Emma never did an inside voice well. "Can't say I'm surprised. Cute house. Cute boyfriend. You even have a creek in the backyard."

Even with all those pluses, it was a minus to be apart from her bestie. "You're welcome to stay with me anytime."

"I can be there in a day." The way Emma drove, she could be in Tennessee in an hour. "Will you find a new oncologist and have breast reconstruction before you begin a new job? I'll take vacation time and be your nurse."

Sam suppressed a laugh. Nursing wasn't in

Emma's skill set, but her friend had a heart almost as big as the blow-up Santa in the yard across the street. "I'm going to wait." Speaking those few words with finality lifted fifty pounds of pressure from Sam's psyche. She didn't have to meet anyone's expectations but her own. "It's not a big deal with Cole, and the surgeon said I could have the surgery anytime." Day by day, it was becoming a lesser deal. "I don't want any complications when I find a new teaching position."

"If things progress and you go on a honeymoon, tell him the absence of your breast makes a comfortable headrest. Ooh, extra points for rhyming."

"Emma!" she blurted. "I'm making lasagna with Cole's mom."

"Just speakin' my truth. I'm sure his mom would like grandbabies." Emma was making her blush. Balloon Santa rocked forward on the breeze as if he was agreeing with Emma.

Sam leaned against the front doorframe. A sweet, ashy fragrance filled the air from one of the neighbor's fireplaces. The aroma reminded Sam of winter in Wisconsin. "Please tell me you'll come for Christmas." Sam's heart ached for Emma. Emma had to balance her faith in God with unbelieving parents who researched every spiritual force but the One True God.

"Of course. Dana and Merilea will be busy marking down candles for the day after Christmas sale. Evergreen Enchantment and Gingerly Gingerbread will be history. My boss has been in and out of the office lately, so he won't mind if I take an extra day." A gush of wind sounded through the phone. "I'm so there. It will be nice to talk openly about Jesus and not have to go to church by myself."

Sam hugged herself to stay warm. "I love you, Em." Sam's throat grew thick. "I couldn't have made it through the cancer and Ted's death without you."

"Sure you could. God brought you through everything. Not to mention your fab folks and the church. I tied up the loose ends." Even Emma's voice warbled.

After saying good-bye to Emma, Sam returned to the kitchen to assist Linda. Cole should have made it to the hospital by now after stopping to get a new phone. She prayed Wade would accept his brother back into the business. The way she saw it, with his injuries, Wade didn't have much of a choice.

~*~

Cole pushed the elevator button for the third floor. Wade had been moved from the surgical ward. In the past week, Cole had prayed for his brother's recovery multiple times. He also petitioned God for wisdom on his relationship with Sam. And then he confessed about getting off track in his faith by chasing Jillie Lynn and her quest for stardom. *I can do everything through Christ who gives me strength.* He grinned and thanked the Lord for his mom's faithfulness in sending devotional booklets.

"Lord, please help me navigate this business expansion with my dad and brother." Cole knocked on

Wade's hospital room door and entered.

Wade's leg was still elevated, and a new cast had appeared on his arm. Dad rested in the lounger by the bed. Both averted their gaze from the television screen. Sports analysis filled the room instead of a beeping monitor.

"Look who's here." Dad leaned forward on the seat cushion and silenced the television.

"You'd better be ready to take Glen's call." Wade shifted in his bed.

Cole dismissed his brother's crankiness with a flip of his hand. "My cell works as well here as in Sperry's Crossing." Only since he'd replaced his boiled phone. "No need to worry, bro." Cole's tone was total chill. That tone received an eye roll from his brother. "I already got the call. Donoven and Son 2.0 is a go."

Wade jerked forward in the bed and winced. His dad rounded the bed frame and grabbed Cole's jacket, pulling him into a side hug with a pat on the back.

"I thought we weren't getting the news until Monday." Wade glanced at the sports stats on the screen before bestowing his full attention.

"We weren't. And Glen wants us to keep quiet until tomorrow afternoon. He thought we might need extra time to sort out logistics due to your accident."

His dad steadied himself with the bed rail. "When did you hear?"

A simple question to stir a hornet's nest. Cole knew his dad didn't mean to start trouble. The smile on his dad's face and the glow of pride radiating from his expression made Cole's chest expand threefold.

Cole scrubbed a hand through his hair. A habit he would have to change or risk going bald. "Yesterday, but I wanted to tell you both in person."

"What was wrong with last night?" The condemnation in Wade's question sent a shiver across Cole's arms.

"Lower your voice, son."

Cole didn't need his dad to referee anymore. Cole had stepped up when the presentation was thrust on him, and he alone nailed it. But staring at his stoic older brother immobile in a hospital bed, the need to defend himself and recount the accolades about his reconnaissance evaporated. God had this scenario all planned out before Cole stepped foot in the doublewide trailer.

"I was busy with Sam. I promised to help her with her house." He wouldn't mention that the help involved decorating for Christmas. "Besides, your bid is solid, and I've already scouted places to live in Sperry's Crossing. We're good." He reached for Wade's uninjured arm and squeezed. "Focus on getting better so you can boss me around. I'll handle the project until you're back on your feet."

"Funny." Wade's lopsided grin gave Cole hope that someday he'd see a full-face smile. "You must have done a decent job pitching my work. Thanks."

Cole branded Wade's thank you into his memory. "You're welcome. You know what they say. Practice makes permanent."

The door to Wade's room opened. His dad held the door for a nurse pushing a food cart.

"Your dinner's here, Mr. Donoven."

Cole placed a hand on his dad's shoulder. "Mom wants us home for dinner. She's making lasagna with Sam."

"Must be nice." Wade inched higher in the bed as the nurse placed the bedside table in front of him.

Doubly nice. Mom's cooking and Sam's presence.

His dad pointed to a tin on the windowsill. "Don't forget your jalapeno peanut brittle. I'm sure your mother will bring you some lasagna tomorrow."

Before Cole followed his dad into the hallway, he said, "I'm praying for you, bro." He truly was, for with each prayer some of the hurt from past years vanished.

Wade cast a glance his direction as the nurse opened Wade's juice. "Don't be a stranger."

Cole nodded. "I won't." In the hallway of a hospital, a few old relational scars healed with the help of God's Son.

~*~

A melody of bells greeted Cole and his dad as they exited the hospital. Young boys huddled behind a table of bagged mistletoe while a parent summoned visitors with two handbells. He could picture Sam corralling kids to sell items for a school event.

"Would you like to buy some mistletoe and support our troop?" a boy asked.

Cole elbowed his dad. "I'm in."

He found the largest bag of mistletoe with the largest red bow and went to pay. His dad had a bag of mistletoe nestled under his arm while he received change from one of the scouts.

"Hey, Dad, I've got this. I only need one bag."

Grinning like a lovesick teenager, his dad said, "Who said this bag's for you?"

Cole laughed. Maybe he wasn't the only electrician in the family creating a few sparks.

~*~

After a delicious dinner, Sam zipped her coat and clasped Cole's hand for a stroll around the neighborhood. Balloon Santa continued his wave from across the street, but his jolliness was eclipsed by the icicle lights cascading from the rooftop.

She could have floated down the sidewalk after hearing that Wade was somewhat cordial and accepting of Cole spearheading the new business venture located near her new home. She was ready to see what plans God had for her in Whispering Creek.

Cole swung her arm as the glow of Christmas lights dazzled the darkness

"Hey, look." Cole directed her toward a tree growing on a strip of grass between the sidewalk and the street. Brightly colored lights zig-zagged through the branches. "What do you know? There's mistletoe in this tree."

Sam studied the leaves and berries. "And what do you know? This mistletoe grew with a red bow on top." She raised her eyebrows and shot him a dubious look. "I've been set up."

"Well, I could have kissed you in the porch light." Cole centered himself under the berries.

"With your parents inside and wavy Santa across the street? Nah." She joined him under the mistletoe. "This is way more private and festive."

Next to a border of glowing candy canes, and under spheres of twinkling lights, without a thought about cancer or reconstruction, she received her best kiss. Ever.

31

CHRISTMAS EVE

Cole breathed in the aroma of mouth-watering turkey. The smoker would have dinner ready in half an hour. He stood next to the rounded grill and near the charred rocks of the firepit where he and Sam had roasted wieners. In three weeks, Sam had become one of his best friends and something more.

Speaking of his significant other, she sauntered around the corner from the front of the house sporting a new navy coat.

"Smells good." She kissed him on the cheek. He was getting use to her kisses. "I came to get an estimated arrival time for the turkey. Our moms are antsy to bake their side dishes. Emma's peeling potatoes."

"I'm guessing one o'clock. The meat should sit for a while after I take it off the heat."

"I second that." His dad strode toward him and Sam. He had two packages tucked under his arms against his down vest. "I'm glad I caught you two together and alone. I have something for you." His dad held out the gifts.

Sam tentatively accepted the present. "You didn't have to bring me anything." Her eyes grew wide as she felt what was inside the wrapping. "I think I know what this is."

Cole had no clue what was inside except that it was collapsible. He tore off the wrapping and shook his head at the Donoven and Son promotional cap. "Dad, I have one of these. I even gave one to Sam."

"You didn't give her one like this." His dad rocked forward on his loafers and brought forth another hat from his back pocket. "I have the original prototype right here." Adjacent to the *n* in *Son* on the baseball cap was a big fancy S written in black marker.

Sam's mouth gaped. The expression on her face mirrored a student being caught writing graffiti on the teacher's desk.

His dad placed the cap on his head. "It's about time we changed our company name, don't you think?"

Cole stared at the cap in his hand. The embroidery on the front read Donoven and Sons Electric. Pressure built behind his eyes. A simple letter had him speechless. He swallowed past years of hurt. "Why now?" Cole glanced at his dad who was wiping his eyes with a handkerchief. A tear traveled down Cole's cheek.

Clearing his throat, his dad came closer, placing a hand on Cole's shoulder. "Sperry's Crossing would have been a lost opportunity if you hadn't stepped up." His dad looked to Sam who held the cap in front of her mouth. Her hazel eyes, awash with emotion, peeked over the top. "And the prototype came in the mail with a note about how hard you were working. I believe Sam gave you an A plus for effort."

Sam sniffled and shoved the hat over her light brown hair. "I had to have something to do while I waited for you to ace the pitch."

Cole traced the soft threads of the company's new name. "I don't know what to say. This is the best Christmas gift. Thank you, Dad." Cole hugged his dad and let years of resentment blow away on the wind with the turkey smoke.

His dad held on tight after Cole loosened his embrace. "I'm proud of you, son. I should have done this years ago. I'm sorry if you thought I didn't appreciate you, because I do, and I did. You're an excellent electrician, and I couldn't have asked for a better son."

Closing his eyes, Cole allowed tears to warm his face. "I love you, Dad."

Sam edged toward the porch and hooked a thumb in the direction of the front door. "I'm going inside before I look like a raccoon."

"Oh, no, you don't." Before Sam could shift another foot and escape, Cole broke the hug with his dad and wrapped her in his arms. "You're the best. Thanks for believing in me," he whispered.

"Better than an A plus?" She shot him a sassy smile.

Cole gave her a discreet kiss. "Much better than an A plus. And much more exciting than a dinosaur sticker."

~*~

Sam held Cole's hand as they strolled from Gretta and Ernie's house. Cole had smoked a smaller turkey for their neighbors in trade for more red-hot gingerbread men. Gretta and Ernie's son was supposed to be arriving soon for Christmas Eve dinner. Sam couldn't remember meeting Jedediah when the family came to visit Ted and Nan in Milwaukee.

Cole's parents had headed back to Nashville. Wade was staying in their house temporarily while he recovered. Mike and Linda didn't want to be gone too long. A coworker had stopped by to keep Wade company.

When they reached the main road the headlights of the UTV blinded her. She blinked at the brightness. Her dad drove the utility vehicle with Mom in the passenger seat. Emma rode in the tailgate.

"Take us up the mountain, Mr. Williams," Emma shouted. Her bestie waved from the back. "You've got half an hour, troubadour, and I want an encore presentation."

Sam waved to her family and cast a glance at Cole. "What is she talking about?"

"Your Christmas gift." Cole rubbed a hand over his jaw. She would have sworn he was blushing, but the setting sun cast too many shadows.

As they made their way toward her home, two chairs had been set near the rescued Christmas tree stationed in front of the porch. A guitar case rested next to one of the seats. Twinkling lights from the tree and strings of bulbs decorating her porch turned the cozy setting into a festive garden.

"Let me guess. You're singing me a song?" She playfully bumped into Cole, relishing the heat emanating from his thick hoodie.

Loud rumbles from a motorcycle grew closer.

"Well, I was." Cole scowled in the direction of the loud noise.

The mechanical roar crossed the bridge. She recognized the raucous purr of a Harley.

"Someone must be lost." Cole shifted in front of her as the biker slowed and drove their direction.

Dressed in black leather pants and a dark jacket with black boots the size of Canada, the rider blended in with the evening. He stopped a few feet from her and Cole, and removed his black metal helmet.

She squeezed Cole's hand as a chill washed over her body.

"Merry Christmas. You must be Cole and Samantha," the rider said.

Her muscles relaxed. This was definitely not the greeting she expected. Where had they met this man before?

"Yes, we are." Cole placed his loose hand on his hip and squared his shoulders. His lawman look was back on display.

"I wanted to thank you for helping my folks out with the storm a while back. It's great they have caring new neighbors. I can't get up here as often as I like." The rider ran a hand through long black hair. "You probably don't recognize me, Sam. I'm Jedediah Beckman. I don't think we met when my family came to Milwaukee. Teen guy, and all."

She drew Cole closer to the bike. If she had to pick Gretta and Ernie's son out of a line up, Jedediah would be the last guy she chose.

"We've enjoyed getting to know Ernie and Gretta. They're wonderful." Sam hoped her voice relayed how fond she was of his parents. The bumpy beginnings had turned into sky gliding.

Cole released her hand. "We just dropped off a smoked turkey."

"I'd better get going. I'm already late." He strapped on his helmet. "Thanks again, and merry Christmas."

"Merry Christmas." She and Cole echoed.

Exhaust fumes tainted the night air.

Cole picked her up and whisked her toward the beckoning Christmas tree lighting up the front of her home. "I don't want any more interruptions. I need to play your song before the UTV returns."

Sam giggled as he bounded for two chairs keeping their glowing pine company. At least he wasn't dropping her in a bathtub.

Hugging herself, she leaned forward in her seat as Cole readied his guitar. Her memory brought back the Scripture she and Cole had read.

Do not be anxious about anything, but in everything, by prayer and petition, with thanksgiving, present your requests to God. And the peace of God, which transcends all understanding, will guard your hearts and your minds in Christ Jesus.

Tears filled her eyes. For the first time in a long time, she was at peace. At peace with her decision to stay in Tennessee. At peace with how she looked. At peace with her job prospects. At peace with the man strumming a tune she should be listening to. And definitely at peace with God for providing everything she didn't know she needed.

A star brightened and faded in the night sky. *Thank you, Ted. For loving and remembering the little girl next door.*

"Samantha Williams." Cole brought her back into the moment. "I know it's only been a few weeks, but every word in this song is true." The reflection in his eyes from the Christmas tree lights was beyond breathtaking. He cleared his throat. "Oh, woman, you may not know, but..."

It's a love ballad. She was twinkling inside all the way to her ankles.

Cole beheld her like she was the only woman in Tennessee and strummed faster.

~*~

"You're the red hots in my sugar cookies, you're the sriracha on my wings, you're the chili in my chocolate, you make my spirit sing." Cole started off softly and then got bolder. "When we talked of life and love, on a hot winter night, I knew deep down in my soul, that you might be my campfire light."

Laughing and crying at the same time, Sam held praying hands over her face.

"So let me in dear Samantha, let me into your life." Cole stopped the song. "Oops. That's the refrain. I've got to save the next line for later."

"Oh, no, you don't. Let me see those lyrics." Sam wiped wetness off her cheeks.

"They're in my head." Cole pointed to his temple. "But what could rhyme with life? Hmm."

"Cole Donoven!" Her heart ricocheted in her chest.

"Shall I go on?" He rocked backward as though he enjoyed making her wait. "The next part is really good. It's about bland cookies." He bestowed the wink that she treasured.

She couldn't help but laugh, enraptured by this man and his sweet song. His love and acceptance made it easier for her to triumph over life's setbacks.

"Take a chance on this troubadour, the one with the wounded heart. I'll give you more than you've ever imagined, to heal your cinnamon, red hot heart." He stopped strumming and gave her that irresistible smile. "Let's make some sugar cookies, woman, and eat them all night long, laughing and talking and composing, a life full of lazy love songs."

Placing his guitar in its case, Cole asked, "What do you think of your gift?"

Before he could ask another question, she leapt from her seat and held his grinning face firmly in her hands. She kissed him. A great, big Christmas-with-all-the-trimmings kiss. And it was definitely electric.

A note from the author

Thank you for reading Sam and Cole's story. You may be wondering why I made Samantha a breast cancer survivor. Here's the reason why.

Back in 2015, I was enjoying a mountain top experience. My first book had been contracted, and eight years of hard work was finally finding success. The theme to my novel was God is in control even in the chaos of life. Little did I know that I would live my book's theme in the form of a battle with breast cancer.

My journey started with a phone call in January. The mammography center called to schedule my annual mammogram. "Oh, by the way," the scheduler said. "We have new 3D imaging. It might cost you fifty dollars if insurance doesn't cover it. Would you like 3D mammography?"

"Sure." My unenthusiastic answer would save my life.

Most ladies agree that mammograms are no fun. The experience is even worse when something is detected. I was summoned from the lounge and called back for additional imaging. Uh-oh, something had shown up on the million-dollar 3D imaging. I waited in the imaging center to have an ultrasound so the "spot" could be confirmed and further imaged.

The ultrasound technician couldn't find my spot. A disgruntled radiologist stormed into the room, and he couldn't find the mysterious shadow. Then a young intern was called to further scan my breast. Dr.

Dreamy didn't find anything either.

False alarm? The consensus was for me to return in six months for another mammogram.

I really didn't give the "spot" much more thought as I had book edits coming, and the publishing business was my new shiny penny.

What I know now, is the spot was a tiny portion of a cancer tumor. Why it didn't show up on the ultrasound still baffles me. What is also baffling is that a tiny portion of the tumor showed up, but not the entirety of the mass. Why was the rest of the tumor invisible? God only knows.

Life lesson #1, don't postpone additional screenings or a biopsy if something shows up on your mammogram. My cancer clock was ticking, and I didn't even know it.

When July rolled around, I had another 3D mammogram at the same center. My spot was still present on the mammography. The ultrasound showed nothing like before, but this time around, the disgruntled radiologist panicked. He wanted a biopsy straightaway.

"Why couldn't you have panicked six months ago?" I felt like saying.

I've been a Christian since the third grade. My faith is important to me. I'm involved in a church and one of the first things I did was start the church prayer chain. Some of my favorite Bible verses are Philippians 4:6-7 (Sam and Cole read these verses).

"Do not be anxious about anything, but in everything, by prayer and petition, with thanksgiving, present your

requests to God. And the peace of God which transcends all understanding will guard your hearts and your minds in Christ Jesus."

September had arrived by the time I got in for a biopsy. My husband and I drove forty-five minutes to a hospital that had a 3D biopsy machine. Remember at the time, 3D imaging was new technology, and the only imaging to pick up that nagging "spot." In order to sample the tumor, the radiologist had to find the mass. Unbeknownst to me, cancer had gotten a nine-month head start. I, however, was still ignorant and praying like mad that this was a false alarm. A malfunction of "new" technology.

The call came five days later at dinner time. I can remember what I was cooking. Spaghetti was on the menu, and I was browning ground beef. I picked up the phone, and the nurse told me that I had breast cancer. The floor in my kitchen had become a bouncy house. I slogged between stirring my meat and grabbing a pen to write my diagnosis on paper.

"Don't worry," the nurse said. "It's small."

I wrote "it's small" on my notepad.

God is in control even in the chaos of life.

The whirlwind of cancer began.

I was referred to a local research hospital and I saw a surgeon.

More scans, including an MRI, confirmed that this was stage 0 cancer. Tiny. I was blessed. All I needed was a lumpectomy and radiation. The dreaded chemotherapy wasn't necessary. Praise the Lord! I could do this. I had "small cancer."

My cover art came for my novel.

More edits—round two—to finish.

Cancer wouldn't stop my dream of being a published author. Or would it?

In October of 2015, I went in for a lumpectomy. In one of my pre-surgery visits, the surgeon had asked me to draw a family tree and write any cancers that my extended family had battled. Being a creative person, I color-coded the cancers. My family tree became a jewel-toned rainbow.

I am thankful that I was at a breast cancer center at a top-rated facility—Froedtert and the Medical College of Wisconsin Hospital. I was able to have genetic testing to determine if this tumor was a fluke or possibly a wake-up call.

As I waited to have my lumpectomy, the surgeon came with my genetic results. I carried a genetic mutation called BRCA-1. Would this change my lumpectomy into a mastectomy or double mastectomy? It may have, but I was gleefully cheering my tiny tumor. God had this covered. I wasn't changing course.

Lumpectomy-radiation-yearly monitoring. My ship readied to sail.

Life lesson #2, if your family tree lights up with a variety of cancer, consider getting genetic testing. BRCA-1 is no laughing matter. Having this genetic mutation increased my rate of having breast cancer to 50-80%, ovarian cancer to 24-40% and pancreatic cancer to 3%.

Surgery is no fun, but all in all, my lumpectomy

went well. The tiny tumor had been removed from my body. My anxiety level dropped. I was ready to get on with life and launch a book in about a year (Yes, traditional publishing is slow).

God was in control. I didn't have to be anxious. I could speed onward with my life and glimpse cancer in my rearview mirror.

After a successful lumpectomy, I envisioned a clean bill of health. I expected the surgeon to say,

"Barb, you're cancer-free. We removed the tumor, and there were clean edges all around."

What did my surgeon truly say?

"Barb, you still have cancer. There was cancer in everything we removed. The tumor was bigger than expected."

How could this be with twenty-first century 3D imaging? Breast MRIs, scans, and mammography?

My eyes stung with tears. I heard words like double mastectomy, oophorectomy, chemotherapy, radiation mapping, reconstruction.

I believe God is in control, I did that day, and I still believe it to this day. But in the surgeon's office, on that day, I cried. I didn't even know what I was supposed to do next. I left the breast cancer center in a haze of disbelief.

Will I even live to see my first book published? God, You're not going to take me home before my launch day, are You? And what about my family, my husband, and children? Don't they need me?

The next day, I woke up and called my surgeon's office. I needed to know the next steps. The nurse told me they were waiting to see what option I had chosen. I remember my response, "I'm going for survival." I was fifty years old and not ready to let cancer win. I would fight. Radical as it might be, I was going all in. Fool me once cancer, but you're not fooling me twice.

I decided on a double mastectomy, an oophorectomy (removal of my ovaries), and no reconstruction. The rate of recurrence with BRCA-1 is 27%. This was my second cancer surgery in two months, and I pray, I will not have to have a third. I'm typing this in 2022. God has granted me more time on earth, but not a day goes by that I don't praise Him for the extra time. I've lost too many loved ones to cancer—my dad, my sister-in-law, an aunt, my grandmother, and close friends. Never underestimate cancer.

Life lesson #3, when you wake up each morning, praise God.

For a story note, Samantha is twenty-three in my novel and doesn't carry a breast cancer genetic mutation, and she doesn't have a family history of breast cancer. Sam felt a lump in her breast. Her reconstruction did not go as planned, but she can have reconstruction in the future. The surgery would be more involved, but it is possible. Could I have reconstruction in the future? I could, but probably won't. I have lived seven years as a breast-free woman, and with my BRCA-1 mutation, I have decided to stay breast-free. I won't say it isn't challenging at times. I could write a story entitled, "Losing My Breasts in the Milwaukee Airport."

"Do not be anxious about anything."

Prayers of the saints were going up on my behalf.

I was praying. Trying to stay strong. Knowing, truly knowing, that God was in control in the chaos of my life.

On December 9, 2015, I underwent a seven-hour surgery to remove my breasts and ovaries. If I had desired reconstruction, the surgeons could have done that as well, but the surgery time would have been extended by several hours.

When I woke from recovery, late on a Wednesday night, I was wheeled to my room. Exhaustion reigned in my body. I stared at my phone on the bedside table and didn't even have the energy to type on Facebook that I was alive. I delegated that job to my husband.

God was faithful. I didn't feel any pain. I walked out of the hospital on Friday morning, with four drains in my chest, still pain-free, and feeling fine. That, my friends, was a miracle of God. Another miracle was that nine days later, I went to my son's college graduation and hosted a small party in his apartment (Without my breast drain attachments).

And as I rested after my surgery, the galley of my book came, and I had ten days to search the manuscript for any errors. If there are errors in "Providence: Hannah's Journey," I blame them on surgery fatigue. During my recovery, I enjoyed yummy meals from my church family.

Life lesson #4, do not suffer in silence. Let your friends and family love on you—with meals, cards, rides, and flowers.

Was my journey over? Hardly.

First came physical therapy so I could reach my arms over my head (A motion needed for radiation therapy).

Second came six weeks of radiation therapy.

Notice I didn't say chemotherapy.

My "tiny" tumor was given an oncotypeDX test. This a test you want to fail. On a scale of 0-100, you want your tumor to be below eighteen. I was a sixteen.

Sixteen. A slower growing tumor. What would my journey have looked like if I had a fast-growing tumor and had waited nine months for a biopsy? The Lord had watched over me. My cancer hadn't left my breast. With no lymph node involvement, I could skip chemotherapy and go straight to my radiation therapy.

Shortly after all my cancer treatments were behind me, I learned my publisher, Pelican Book Group, planned to release my novel in October of 2016. October is Breast Cancer Awareness Month. In October of 2015, I was newly diagnosed with breast cancer. In October of 2016, I was a breast cancer survivor. My publisher had no idea of my struggles.

I lived each day in the peace that only God can give. Whether God gave me more days on this earth or took me home, I knew He was in control.

God is in control even in the chaos of life. I pray you have this faith in God, too.

Thank you for reading both of my stories. One fiction, and one real.

Psalm 46:1-2:

God is our refuge and strength, an ever-present help in

trouble.

Therefore we will not fear, though the earth give away and the mountains fall into the sea,"

Or as Cole would say: *"I can do everything through Christ who gives me strength."* Philippians 4:13

Acknowledgements

This book would not have been possible without the help of so many people. My family has been the best cheering section throughout my publishing career. I am blessed to have their love, encouragement, and support.

A big thank you goes to my editor, Fay Lamb, who helped improve Cole and Samantha's story and to Nicola Martinez who has made my books a reality for readers.

My critique partners cheered me on while writing this story. Without their input, these pages would not shine as bright. Thank you, Sandy Goldsworthy, Olivia Rae, and Kathy Zdanowski.

The author communities of ACFW, RWA, SCBWI, and my publisher Pelican Book Group, have been a huge support in my writing career. The original Barnes & Noble Brainstormers continue to encourage my spirit. Thank you, Jill Bevers, Karen Miller, Betsy Norman, and Sandra Turriff. These ladies also supported me through my cancer journey.

My church family has kept me going during good times and bad. What a blessing to have their loving support. My church prayed for me faithfully during my cancer journey and brought me delicious meals.

I will always be grateful to the oncologists who brought me through cancer. Dr. Alonzo Walker, Dr. John Burfeind, Dr. Carmen Bergom, and Dr. Erin Bishop gave me the best care. The nurses at the Breast Cancer Center at Froedtert were amazing. Thank you,

Anna Purdy, Cheryl, Kimberly Roller-Voight, and to the caring staff.

I want to thank Gale Pearson for the wise counsel of practice makes permanent. Both my boys learned this saying in Ms. Pearson's third grade class.

I'm grateful to Burki Electric for answering my electrical questions.

And last, but not least, praise to The Lord God Almighty, for giving me the gift of creativity and breath each day to write these stories. I am a cancer survivor, and not a day goes by that I don't praise the Lord for his healing. To God be the glory.

If you would like more information about breast cancer, my cancer center recommends these websites:

American Cancer Society: www.cancer.org
Young Survival Coalition: www.youngsurvival.org
(More and more women in their twenties and thirties are getting breast cancer. Since mammography usually starts later in life, these women usually feel the lump in a monthly breast check. This was Sam's situation in my novel).

Thank you

We appreciate you reading this White Rose Publishing title. For other inspirational stories, please visit our on-line bookstore at www.pelicanbookgroup.com.

For questions or more information, contact us at customer@pelicanbookgroup.com.

White Rose Publishing
Where Faith is the Cornerstone of Love™
an imprint of Pelican Book Group
www.PelicanBookGroup.com

Connect with Us
www.facebook.com/Pelicanbookgroup
www.twitter.com/pelicanbookgrp

To receive news and specjals, subscribe to our bulletin
http://pelink.us/bulletin_

May God's glory shine through
this inspirational work of fiction.

AMDG

You Can Help!

At Pelican Book Group it is our mission to entertain readers with fiction that uplifts the Gospel. It is our privilege to spend time with you awhile as you read our stories.

We believe you can help us to bring Christ into the lives of people across the globe. And you don't have to open your wallet or even leave your house!

Here are 3 simple things you can do to help us bring illuminating fiction™ to people everywhere.

1) If you enjoyed this book, write a positive review. Post it at online retailers and websites where readers gather. And share your review with us at reviews@pelicanbookgroup.com (this does give us permission to reprint your review in whole or in part.)

2) If you enjoyed this book, recommend it to a friend in person, at a book club or on social media.

3) If you have suggestions on how we can improve or expand our selection, let us know. We value your opinion. Use the contact form on our web site or e-mail us at customer@pelicanbookgroup.com

God Can Help!

Are you in need? The Almighty can do great things for you. Holy is His Name! He has mercy in every generation. He can lift up the lowly and accomplish all things. Reach out today.

Do not fear: I am with you; do not be anxious: I am your God. I will strengthen you, I will help you, I will uphold you with my victorious right hand.

~Isaiah 41:10 (NAB)

We pray daily, and we especially pray for everyone connected to Pelican Book Group—that includes you! If you have a specific need, we welcome the opportunity to pray for you. Share your needs or praise reports at http://pelink.us/pray4us

Free eBook Offer

We're looking for booklovers like you to partner with us! Join our team of influencers today and periodically receive free eBooks!

For more information
Visit http://pelicanbookgroup.com/booklovers